FIVE DAYS TO KILL A MAN

She scrambled at her clothing, coming up with her derringer.

"Vivian!" Tallman shouted as he reached for the small gun she pointed at Traber. He firmly grasped her hand and she moved the gun away. "We need him alive."

Vivian loosened her grip and let Tallman take the derringer. She wanted to encircle him with her arms and cry for two hours, but she bit her lip and held strong.

"Jesus Christ, Viv," Tallman said as he looked down. Her whole body from her knees to her face was criss-crossed with red welts. Catching his eyes, she looked down too. She cradled her breast and examined the two small burns.

"I'm sorry, Viv," Tallman said.

"I'll heal. Just be glad you got here when you did. He was about to get rough."

"Traber," Tallman said as he looked toward the man, and Vivian began to dress. "You better pray you hang. Cause if you don't, I'm going to show you how it can take five days to kill a man."

ST. MARTIN'S PAPERBACKS TITLES
BY MATT BRAUN

Black Fox
Outlaw Kingdom
Lords of the Land
Cimarron Jordan
Bloody Hand
Noble Outlaw
Texas Empire
The Savage Land
Rio Hondo
The Gamblers
Doc Holliday
You Know My Name
The Brannocks
The Last Stand
Rio Grande
Gentleman Rogue
The Kincaids
El Paso
Indian Territory
Bloodsport
Shadow Killers
Buck Colter
Kinch Riley
Deathwalk
Hickok & Cody
The Wild Ones
Hangman's Creek
Jury of Six
The Spoilers
Manhunter
The Warlords
Deadwood
The Judas Tree
Black Gold
The Highbinders
Crossfire

CROSSFIRE

MATT BRAUN

St. Martin's Paperbacks

Previously published as *Ash Tallman: Crossfire* by Tom Lord (a pseudonym for Matt Braun).

CROSSFIRE

Library of Congress Catalog Card Number: 84-90793

ISBN: 0-312-99785-X
EAN: 80312-99785-3

Printed in the United States of America

Avon Books edition / April 1984
St. Martin's Paperbacks edition / September 2004

St. Martin's Paperbacks are published by St. Martin's Press, 175 Fifth Avenue, New York, NY 10010.

10 9 8 7 6 5 4 3 2 1

CROSSFIRE

ONE

Iron rails creaked and popped as a short train, drawn by a No. 4 Baldwin, swayed and rattled toward the distant depot, leaving a trail of hot cinders and black smoke. A brassy sun floated high in the cloudless sky, its strident rays outlining the tall dark pines that carpeted the purple ridges of the Sangre de Cristo Mountains. Nestled in the mile-high folds, Santa Fe, the territorial capital of New Mexico, appeared out of place as the buff-white walls of the town's adobe buildings shimmered in waves of heat.

As their compartment car shuddered along the steel ribbons, Ash Tallman and Vivian Valentine sat quietly, lulled by the clickety-click of steel on steel and the rhythmic sound of chugging pistons.

"Another half hour," Tallman noted as he stretched his long legs and yawned. "And we'll be on our way to the hotel."

"Back to work," Vivian said, frowning and pouting in jest. "I won't have you to myself any longer."

Tallman raised one eyebrow and allowed a thin smile.

Vivian liked that gesture. It somehow fit the tall and handsome Pinkerton detective. His rugged and angular features were dominated by a determined jaw and steel-gray eyes, which seemed to mirror his unique character.

"Oh, we might get together from time to time," Tallman added. "We'll wrap this one up and take our good old time on the trip back to Chicago."

Vivian studied him for a moment, and then rose from her seat. She settled beside him on the plush, velvet-covered couch that folded out to provide narrow sleeping accommodations.

"This is better," she purred. "You're right. It shouldn't be much work to catch a few stagecoach robbers."

"Might not be that easy," Tallman said as he fished a thin cheroot from his jacket pocket. "From what Allan Pinkerton told me, these highwaymen are not your garden-variety thieves. But we'll know more before the day's out."

"Hell," Vivian sighed. "They don't stand a chance with us."

Tallman's eyes twinkled at her self-assured words. She was a spitfire, a one-of-a-kind woman who threw all convention to the wind, especially when it came to the pleasures of the forbidden fruit. Though he'd laid his eyes on her nude form many times in the past several months, he was still taken aback by the sight of her statuesque frame, full breasts, and lissome legs. She carried herself erect, in the manner of a great lady. And when she smiled, she could sap the chill from a January blizzard.

"They probably don't," he said as he scratched a sulphurhead on his bootheel. "Of course," he added, drawing on the cigar and allowing a serious tone. "They've killed two drivers already . . . in cold blood."

"The wages of sin is death," she said, her eyes lighting up the compartment.

Tallman shook his head. He mused that this bright and articulate woman had a never-ending supply of good humor and bawdy wit. And she seemed unaffected by life's imponderables. Gas-bag politicians, fevered-brow Bible thumpers, hardened thieves, drunks and bums, greedy robber barons, and the mass of people living lives of quiet desperation were all, from her perspective on life, as much a part of the scheme of things as the wind, the sand, and the stars. She usually shrugged her shoulders at the bizarre. They didn't know it then, but the days ahead would push Vivian to her limits.

A shrill hoot from the Baldwin's whistle signaled the end of their journey from Chicago.

Tallman stood and stretched as the train began to slow down. "Say so long to the good life for a while," he said as he put his palm on the compartment ceiling to steady himself against the bucking and surging of the decelerating train.

"Nothing wrong with a little adventure. The Grim Reaper will turn us into worm food soon enough. Grab it while you can."

"You'll get no argument from me," the detective replied as he shrugged into his shoulder rig, snatched his .41 Colt New Line from the small shelf next to the seat, and stuffed it into the wet-molded leather hideout rig. "I'd have made a piss-poor hardware drummer."

As Vivian fixed her hair and straightened her clothing, Tallman put on his gray suit-jacket and then retrieved his dead cigar.

"All set?" he asked as the train finally groaned to a halt.

"Santa Fe! San . . . ta Feee!" the porter chanted as he walked the car passageway.

On the station platform they hired a small Mexican boy to carry their bags, and then strolled toward the Plaza de Armas with the ease of lifelong residents. Two blocks after a left on San Francisco Street they arrived at the Santo Domingo Hotel. When they stopped at the desk, the boy set down the bags and thrust his dirty hand forward. Tallman dropped four bits into the outstretched mitt and the kid made a dash for the door, hoping for another run or two.

After Tallman signed the register and paid for one day in advance, they were shown to the room.

"Lunch?" Tallman asked, after the desk clerk had left the room. "I know just the place, and Mr. Oldham will not get here for several hours."

"Lead the way, professor."

Tallman led Vivian to a Mexican restaurant he'd frequented on earlier trips to Santa Fe. For two hours they sampled small plates of spicy delicacies and consumed two bottles of a local white wine. During that time Tallman outlined the case, based on the scanty details he'd gotten from Allan Pinkerton the day before their departure from Chicago. Later that afternoon they were to meet with Perry Oldham, Wells Fargo division superintendent for the Arizona Territory. "It sounds to me that we're dealing with a Judas," Tallman went on after a sip of the fruity wine. "When something goes off this slick time after time, you *have to* assume inside information."

"Who's to say it isn't this Oldham?"

"We can't. But Pinkerton went high up in Wells Fargo for assurances."

"Calculated risk."

Tallman nodded.

"And that's all we have to go on?"

"Until this afternoon," he said as he raised his glass.

"Perry Oldham's my name," the man said when Tallman opened the hotel-room door. "Are you Stephen Barlow of the Chicago Barlows?"

"Sure am," Tallman said as he waved the heavyset man into the room. "Did you keep an eye over your shoulder?" Tallman asked after he closed the door.

"Yes, sir! Made damn certain I had no shadow."

"Ash Tallman," the detective said as he extended his hand and offered a smile. "And this is Vivian Valentine," he said, turning. "My partner."

Oldham shook Tallman's hand with a grip that suggested that his bulk was mostly muscle and then turned and nodded toward Vivian. "Dangerous work for a woman, isn't it?"

"At times, Mr. Oldham," Vivian replied. "But I've been able to hold my own."

"Well I surely do hope you'll watch your step on this case. These bastards have killed four of my best men, two of them personal friends."

"Four?" Tallman injected. "Pinkerton told us two."

"They killed a guard and a driver the day before last, just outside Elroy. Our noon stage to Gila Bend and Yuma. We lost thirty-two thousand in gold and silver." The Wells Fargo man got red-faced at the mention of it. "So, like I said, watch your step."

"Let's sit down and cover the details," Tallman suggested, feeling less concerned about the likelihood that Oldham was, himself, the traitor. The silent rage that had glowed in his cheeks was real. "Whiskey? I had them send up a bottle of the good stuff," Tallman asked, pointing to a fresh bottle of Bull's Head Sourmash.

"I was hopin' you'd ask, Mr. Tallman. All that dust left a lizard in my throat."

"Hang your coat and lid, and I'll pour."

"Let me get it, Mr. Oldham," Vivian insisted as

the Wells Fargo superintendent took off his coat and bowler, revealing a small sidearm sheathed in leather.

When they'd settled in with their drinks, Oldham began his tale, providing dates, places, and a brief description of each holdup. To date, he explained, they'd lost $280,000. "I'll leave my written reports so that you can go over them tonight."

"I'm curious, though," Tallman said. "What about your guards and drivers? Why weren't they able to protect the shipments?"

"They tried, Mr. Tallman," the beefy Oldham replied stiffly, as he slugged the last of his sourmash. "And they're mostly dead."

"Sounds like inside information," Tallman suggested. "Is there any possibility one of your local company men could be working with the gang?"

"Everybody's been checked and rechecked. They're friends and long-time employees," Oldham insisted as he twirled the end of his black handlebar mustache. Then he released a windy sigh. "But everything points to it. We've tried phantom shipments, rerouted shipments, and hidden shipments. They only hit when there's gold, and they always know right where it is."

"Seems pretty clear, Mr. Oldham," Vivian added. "You've got a fox in the chicken coop."

"Whatever I've got, I've got to have these depredations against Wells Fargo stopped."

Vivian poured more whiskey for the two men

without asking whether or not they wanted a refill.

"Any suspects?" Tallman asked.

"Nothing solid, but we have our own Wells Fargo detectives nosing around Tucson and the outlying towns. One of them, Bert Hollins, picked up on a hard case named Doc Stroud. He's a scarfaced bum who always has a lot of gold coin to splash around in Red Rock gaming dives and whorehouses. But that's all Hollins has . . . that and hearsay that he holes up somewhere in the Picacho Mountains."

"Anything else on Stroud's description?" Vivian asked, already assuming that she would set out after *him*.

"Hollins said he figured Stroud was the type who'd shoot his own mother for two bits. Stands six feet. Muscular build and thick through the shoulders. Has a long scar on his left cheek. Red-brown hair. Hollins says you'll spot the mean eyes first."

"Hollins knows about us?"

"No. Of course not," Oldham came back. "No one does."

"Let's keep it that way," Vivian said, her voice sounding concern. "It's our understanding that only you are to know."

"You might say, Mr. Oldham, that we are placing our lives in your hands," Tallman said, his eyes conveying the message that a slip on Oldham's part might be fatal . . . to Oldham himself. "That's a heavy load to haul around . . . if you get my meanin'?"

Oldham nodded complete understanding.

For the next hour the trio discussed further details, including how they were to stay in contact with each other. Tallman explained that he had decided to make no plans for a contact; he simply assured the Wells Fargo man that he'd hear something when there was something to tell. Then they ended their meeting with five minutes of small talk and another sourmash.

As soon as Oldham departed, Vivian reached for the buttons on her dress and began undoing them. "I'm going to the bathhouse and take a nice long hot bath. I assume we leave in the morning."

"You are reading my mind."

"How will we approach the problem?" she asked as she tugged the dress down and began undoing the wire hooks on her corset.

"The only thing we have is Stroud and Red Rock. So we'll start from there," he said, his eyes dropping to her milk-white cleavage. "We'll go in a day apart. You'll pose as a small-time dancehall queen who'd had a run of bad luck. I'll play the part of a hard case on the run."

"Oooo, that feels good," she said as she threw the stiff underwear on the bed and massaged her large breasts with a slow circular motion.

Tallman's eyes moved to her chest. He'd never met a woman with such unabashed views on the nature and purpose of the human body.

"I gather we'll avoid contact until we have reason to communicate," she went on as she squirmed out of her petticoat. She looked up as she threw it on the bed.

Tallman was feasting his eyes on Vivian's almost-nude body.

"I think I'm reading your mind again," she said, vamping him with inviting lips and luminescent eyes. "Or maybe your britches," she added as she came forward and fingered the mound growing out of his gray slacks. "Come to think of it, maybe we'd better communicate now if we're going to be apart for a spell."

"Maybe."

With her other hand she pulled Tallman closer and pressed her soft, moist lips to his, at once probing deeply into his mouth with her sinuous tongue. When the kiss ended, she began with his shirt, making a production of the disrobing while he massaged one of her rosy nipples with thumb and finger.

"Ooo. Good," she groaned as he twirled the hardening nipple. Her hands quickly found his belt buckle and the buttons on his fly.

She bent lower, breaking his grasp on her brown, hard nipple. She tugged on his pants and shorts and let them fall as she went to her knees, her face next to his upright cock.

"God, I love this," she groaned as she took his rigid member gently in both hands and guided it so that the sensitive tip brushed lightly against both of her cheeks. Then she kissed it playfully, causing a faint sucking sound. She opened wide and took the tip into her mouth.

Tallman let out a gusty breath as her tongue spiraled over his throbbing glans and hovered at the tip of the head. He buried his strong fingers in her auburn hair and began to churn his hips. She took him deeper with each gyration until she had all of him in her hot, moist mouth. Making odd animal sounds, she cupped his balls and squeezed with one hand as she fingered the base of his turgid shaft with the other. The tempo of his thrusts was increasing as he was becoming overpowered, with the sensation of her artful tongue and hands. Nearing the point of oblivion, he pushed her away, but she held on and sucked his meat in again to the back of her throat.

Tallman pulled out again, hoisted her aloft, and effortlessly carried her to bed. He quickly removed her panties, garter, and stockings, then kneaded the silken flesh of her inner thighs and gazed at the dew on the auburn hair at the edges of her womanhood. Caught up in the moment, he lowered himself between her legs, closed his lips on the pink petals and worked his tongue, darting in and out of the wet slit.

Vivian's hips shuddered. In moments her squeals rose to an eerie shriek as she writhed and grabbed at the fresh sheets. When her juices began streaming, Tallman suddenly rose, positioned her legs over his shoulders and drove his manhood deep into the pink opening. After his quick penetration, he pulled back slowly. Together they moved in a rocking motion, straining their sensitized bodies in perfect union.

"Yes! Oh God, Ash! Deeper!" she moaned, her eyes closed. Her bucking hips began to pound as sensual moaning turned to guttural sounds and she grabbed the vertical bars on the brass bedstead.

Tallman unleashed a final flurry of thrusts and his seed flooded her insides in decreasing spasms while Vivian made grunting sounds and released waves of her own juice. Their bodies stiffened as they reached the pinnacle and fell into space on the other side.

TWO

A high-wheeled coach rattled and jolted through the ruts in the road. The canvas blinds had been lowered part way to block the blistering sun. Nonetheless, the passengers wilted. Only scrub trees and odd-shaped, rust-colored boulders occasionally interrupted the purple-gray monotony of the Arizona desert. In the distance, sun-bleached board-and-batten buildings danced in the shimmering heat waves.

Red Rock lay near the foot of the mountains, just below Picacho Pass. A white man's town in a hostile land, its inhabitants were a motley group of down-and-outs and a well-entrenched lower element who provided the amusements. Only twenty-five miles from Tucson, the capital of the Arizona Territory, Red Rock was also a stop-off point for thieves, assorted charlatans, and hard-nosed prospectors who worked the desolate mountains.

Vivian's shoulders dropped in relief when the stage

rumbled to a stop. Clad in a low-cut red dress that clashed with her overdone auburn hair, she looked like a fallen woman. The heat and the choppy stage ride had put the crowning touch on her disguise. She *felt* the part. When her feet hit solid ground, she gazed at the dusty main street and the spartan buildings. Across the way she saw a general store flanked by a stable and a ramshackle hotel. Three doors down from the hotel, the Silver Dollar saloon seemed to be the center of activity.

Vivian left her carpetbag in the stage office and told the driver that she would call for it later. On her way to the Silver Dollar, she passed two idlers. While eyeing the men, she pushed her shoulders back and adjusted her floppy, feather-decked hat. Their interested stares followed her hips. Glancing over her shoulder, she smiled to herself, always amused at the way most men would weaken when tempted by the desires of the flesh. Still smiling, she passed the hotel and continued to the saloon. Pausing at the door, she glanced suggestively in the direction of the loafers. When she came through the batwings, she found an uncrowded long bar made of a large rough-sawn timber. Numerous crude wooden tables and chairs were scattered about the room. A big man with a crooked nose and a roll of flesh hanging over his belt sat at one of the tables with an open ledger.

"Hi, there," Vivian said as she approached the man with the ledger. "You own this joint?"

The mean-faced man leaned back, hooked his

thumbs in the pockets of his gold vest, and deliberately focused his eyes on her overflowing bosom.

"Who's askin'?"

"Lizzie Todd."

The man held his eyes on her chest and nodded approval.

"Brought you some business," she said as she glanced over her shoulder in the direction of the two loafers, who had followed her in. "And I figure I could bring in a few more just like them two."

"Name's Chunk Frazer. This here's my place," he answered as he moved his lecherous gaze to her eyes and wiped the corners of his drooping mustache with a large, grubby knuckle. "Lookin' fer work?"

Without an invite, Vivian drew out a chair and sat down. She crossed her legs toward the door and the two idlers who were headed to the bar. The pair gawked a moment, then ordered whiskey.

"Could be," she said as she placed a red-nailed fingertip to her lips and sensuously touched it with her tongue. "If the work's right."

"What's right?" Frazer asked as his eyes darted again to the creamy vee at the top of her dress.

"Most everything . . . except I ain't in the business of droppin' my drawers for just any old stink-ass miner or stiff-dicked cowpoke."

Frazer slid his chair closer and took hold of her elbow. "Well, I might be able to use a woman who can do *most . . . anything.*" Then his fingers crawled up her arm.

"You can see how easy I hustle drinks," she went on as she eased herself back and nodded again toward the pair she'd led into the Silver Dollar. "Led those boys in here neat as you please."

"What else can you do?" he asked. Spittle appeared at the corner of his mouth and his breath reeked of whiskey. "Those old boys hang here all the time anyhow."

"The usual. Roll a drunk. Run a scam. Turn a trick. Whatever you need."

"What I need is what you got hid down there 'tween your legs," Frazer said as he released her arm and grabbed her breast with his other hand. He kneaded her flesh forcefully. "You might work out. But old Chunk don't bring nobody on the payroll 'lessen he's took a close look-see at the prospective employee."

"You'll get a look-see, but on my terms," she growled as she held her face in a hard look. "I say who and when. So if you ain't interested, I seen a couple of waterin' holes up the street that might want to up their whiskey sales." She looked down at his grip on her large breast. "Finished yet?"

"Well, hogshit on my boot! Ain't we got us a wildcat here. No need to get all hot, lady. *You* said you'd open them legs for gold. Didn't see no harm in a free sample. Hell, any good drummer's got free samples," Frazer said in a friendly tone as he released her flesh. "No hurry."

"Most drummers I know don't get sick once a

month either," Vivian shot back after erasing her scowl. "You catch my drift."

"Ohhh," Frazer howled, as he slapped both hands on the ledger book, which was opened wide on the crude table. "No wonder she's so testy." Frazer acted friendly all of a sudden, her words about heading for another saloon still clear in his mind. Red Rock hadn't seen the likes of Lizzie Todd in some time, and he intended to keep her for the Silver Dollar. "Go get cleaned up. I'll have the swamper show you a room out back."

"What about terms?" Vivian insisted. "I want to know where I stand . . . up front."

"Two dollars a day for the girls on nights, split seventy-five–twenty-five on booze, and fifty-fifty on fuck money," Frazer said as he hauled a small dirk from his belt and began cleaning his fingernails. "And no workin' your pussy on the side. That's one thing that ain't good for your health, if you get what I'm sayin'?"

"What about protection for your girls?"

"I'm my own bouncer," he said as he flexed his arms. "Ain't many that cares to tangle with old Chunk."

Vivian figured him for a bull who liked bustin' heads. His bent nose, thick ears, and the layers of scar tissue over his left eye lent credence to the words.

"Bink!" Frazer yelled toward the back of the saloon. "Git your skinny ass in here."

A fourteen-year-old towhead ran from a back room.

"Watcha wan', Mr. Frazer?"

"Bink, show this lady to the empty room," Frazer said as Vivian got up.

"Shore thing!"

Frazer reached up her dress and gently massaged the silky flesh on her inner thigh. The young swamper's face turned crimson. "I'll come by later and see you're settled in. After I do these goddamned accounts," Frazer said, showing her a toothy smirk that exposed several black teeth and rotting gums that made Vivian's own teeth ache.

"I told you, Chunk. It ain't the right time of the goddamn month," she said, faking a playful voice.

"There's more 'n one way to make the one-eyed monster spit fire," Frazer said as he grabbed his crotch with his other hand.

"Come on, Bink," Vivian said to the swamper as she spun out of Frazer's lewd grip. "Show me my room before this bull corrupts your ears beyond redemption."

Frazer grunted and went back to the ledger.

A few minutes later Vivian stood looking at her accommodations. Hardly more than a crib in a back-alley whorehouse, she thought. After slumping on the double bed, which occupied more than half the room, she kicked off her shoes and wiggled her toes. She was pondering her situation and dreading the moment the rotten-mouthed Frazer would demand her flesh. Assured that she'd think of something, she got up and wriggled out of the dusty red dress. She was undoing her corset when she heard a soft rap on the door. Her heart sank as she opened it, expecting to find Chunk Frazer in the hallway.

Bink, the swamper, stood bug-eyed. She'd forgotten that she'd sent him for the carpetbag.

"Thanks, Bink," she said, pointing to the bed. "Put it over there."

Struck dumb, the youngster padded across the worn carpet and deposited the valise on the bed, turned, and stopped, staring at exposed flesh as a strawberry glow spread over his cheeks.

"I'll give you two bits out of my first pay," she said, devilishly pondering the possibility that the boy was virgin.

"Yes'm," he said as he scampered from the dank room.

An hour later, she had splash-bathed in the basin on the rickety dresser and she was applying makeup. War paint, she thought to herself. Carefully, she rouged her cheeks and then painted her mouth into a shiny cupid's bow. As an afterthought, she added a beauty spot at the corner of her left eye. She stood back from the dull mirror and nodded approval. "A real sleaze," she said out loud.

Satisfied, she turned to her carpetbag and drew out a frilly wine-colored peek-a-boo dress that was accented with glass gems. After tending to her glossy auburn hair, she slipped the sheer dress over her head, careful not to smudge her gaudy makeup. Once in place, the dress seemed to ripple with a life of its own. She laughed when she saw the outcome of her effort in the chipped mirror. But as she slipped on black stockings, she momentarily wondered why she was there in Red Rock, Arizona. She hooked one stocking to the garter and stopped. "Why?" she asked the wall. She mused that she could be working a con on some rich city slicker who didn't have rotten teeth and breath like vulture shit. But she recalled the close call she had when Tallman uncovered her game and saved her from a slow death in the New York State Women's Prison. "Why not!" she said, dismissing her question. Same game, different side of the law, she thought to herself. After she rolled on the other stocking and checked her outfit a final time, she left the room.

The sun was still above the horizon, but men had already begun to stream into the Silver Dollar. She paused at the door leading from the saloon to the back rooms and straightened her shoulders. Her breasts swelled like ripe melons over her tight decolletage. Her tiny waist accented her hips and produced an hourglass form. When she entered, drop-jawed drinkers eyed her fruit.

"Hey, honey!" one cowboy, carrying a load of pop-skull, shouted over the clink-clank of an out-of-tune piano. "How's about you and me go back to your room for a little jig-jig!"

"Later, big boy," she answered in a husky voice.

"That is, if you can keep it stiff after what you've put away."

The others at his table roared with laughter as the cowboy to his right thumped the loudmouth's Stetson down to his ears.

The bartender nodded for Vivian's help as he loaded a tray for a table of card slicks. Thus she started an evening that merged into endless hours of fending off horny miners, drunken cowhands, and foul-mouthed riffraff. Her bottom was sore from sly pinches and her feet throbbed in the spike-heeled shoes. Eight o'clock turned to nine, and then to ten. She longed for closing time. Yet she continued to smile, kid the loudmouths with sharp backtalk, and hustle drinks.

Then, near a quarter to eleven, the batwings slammed open and a squint-eyed tough pounded toward the bar, followed by three other hard cases, two older men and a fuzz-faced blond kid who had the devil in his eyes.

"Hey, Doc," someone shouted through lips thick with whiskey. "How ya doin', you goddamned rattlesnake."

"Hey, Leroy," Doc shouted back. "Still fuckin' your sister?"

Vivian turned just as the laughter erupted, when she heard someone shout "Doc."

"Whiskey for me and the boys," the man named Doc said to the harried barkeep. "An' don't try to pawn off any of that Apache juice on *us!*"

After she scanned the room, her eyes locked on the new customer. Oldham's words flashed in her mind. *You'll spot the mean eyes first.* If the whole case goes this good, she thought to herself, we'll bank a heavy fee and be on our way home inside a week.

Doc Stroud and his three sidekicks snatched the bottle of whiskey and the glasses from the bar and headed for a table occupied by a lone drunk. As Stroud passed, Vivian got a closer look. The scar-faced man with mean eyes matched Oldham's description perfectly.

"Hey, Doc," the bearded sidekick said. "Looks like Chunk's hired him a new girl."

Doc stopped and turned. "A might easier on the eyes than Ellie and Aggie," Doc said, referring to the other two women working the floor.

At the table, he hoisted the drunk out of the chair and threw the limp figure on the floor. Again his trio laughed, a chorus of guttural noises.

When she saw the passed-out miner go flying like a sack of oats, she was sure that Stroud *would* cut his mother's throat for six bits. Nevertheless, she fixed a suggestive look on her face, moistened her lips with a twirl of her tongue, and walked straight toward the four thugs.

"Can I get you boys anything?" she asked when she got to the table.

"How about you get another glass and join us," Stroud commanded in a polite voice. "That'd please me just fine."

"Why, thanks," she said.

When she returned, she pulled out a chair and slid the glass forward. The blond fuzzface had the bottle but he held it firm and stared into Vivian's eyes with a kiss-my-ass expression.

"Chrissake, kid," Stroud moaned. "Ain't no call to be a shitass. Pour the lady a drink. No wonder you don't git no women an' have to pull your mouse yourself."

The kid looked at Doc with murder in his eyes and then turned toward Vivian. After a pause, he slid the bottle toward her. She caught it before it left the table, and poured a drink.

"Don't mind him," Stroud said to Vivian. "Indians killed his folks when he was eight and he's been fendin' for hisself ever since."

Vivian slugged back the whole shot, looking forward to the glow it might provide.

"So what's yer name?" the man with the beard asked.

"Lizzie Todd."

"Right nice to meet you," Doc said with the grace of a deacon at a church picnic. "This here's Jake," he added, pointing to the man with the beard. "Kirk," he went on as he nodded toward the other older man. "And then we got our kid here. Kriss Kliegle. A pureblood square-head. Folks come right from Holland or some goddamn place. Doin' all right, too, until the redskins snatched their yellow hair."

"Fuck you, Doc," the kid said as he turned his half-full glass upside down and got up.

"You oughten be so rough on the kid," Kirk said from under his dusty, sweat-stained flat-brim Stetson. "Ain't he had enough bullshit for a lifetime?"

"Likely to gut you some night while you're sleepin'," the bearded Jake warned. "Kid's bad crazy."

Vivian refilled her glass and did likewise for the others.

"Do you boys come here often?" she asked them. "I'm new in town. Haven't made any friends yet."

"We usually have a look-see in the Silver Dollar every now and then," Stroud answered.

"You a real doctor?" she asked Stroud. "I heard 'em call you Doc."

The three men laughed, Stroud the loudest.

"See this scar?" he asked as he ran his finger down the crease in his face. "My own doctorin'. After some Indian cut me right to the bone, I cut his throat and then sewed it up with a needle and the hair from my paint's tail. All without no mirror or nothin'. Somebody called me Doc and it stuck."

"You did a helluva job," she said as she ran her fingertip slowly over the scar. Her smile widened and she looked right into Doc's blue eyes. "Gives you character. . . . Damned if it don't."

Kirk grunted at the babble and tossed his whiskey. Jake followed suit.

"You said you was without friends?" Doc asked.

"My first day in town," Vivian answered.

"Well, now, I do believe you just found yourself one."

"Jake," Kirk grunted. "What say we go over to O'Riley's and find us a card game? Maybe build on our capital stock."

"Now you're thinkin' like a true businessman. We'll just leave these two to their love talk."

"Guess those boys seen I was makin' eyes for you and not them," Vivian said after they left. Then she let her leg rest on Stroud's Levis. "But it looks to me like you're runnin' the show anyhow."

"Might say that."

"I mean, I couldn't help notice that people figure you're *somebody*. The way they looked when you got here."

Stroud straightened in his chair as Vivian continued to carefully pump him up. She asked him questions about his past, his girl friends, and his exploits with the Indians. He belted the whiskey and sang boastful tunes. She'd found the key—his vanity.

"Hell," he said finally. "Here I am spoutin' off, and all I know about you is your name."

"Not much to tell. My folks had me all set to marry the pimple-faced son of some preacher. But I had it in my mind to get away from all those stiff-shirts. And here I am, ten years later."

"What the hell brought you to Red Rock?"

"Seemed like as good a place as any to stay shy of the law dogs for a while."

"You runnin'?"

She hung her head.

Stroud laughed louder than he had all night and poured another glass of rye.

"Wasn't no laughin' matter when we got caught. Expect my partner's right now on his way to the territorial prison in Santa Fe."

"What'd you do?"

"You won't think less of me, will you? You bein' a businessman and all."

"Businessman!"

"Your friends said—"

"Forget them," Stroud interrupted as he put his hand on her leg. "Spin me a yarn. I ain't never knowed but one other lady outlaw, and she don't look like you."

"Wasn't much to it," Vivian went on, her rundown body buoyed by his calling her an outlaw. She guessed she could move in all the sooner. "Peter and me—really, he made me do it—worked a game on preachers." She poured another drink, her glow coming on just right. "We'd come to a town like man and wife, Peter and me. Then we'd get with the church and join in on everything. Picnics. Bible class. Fund raisin'. Peter knew the Bible front-to-back. Well . . . after we was in good, I'd kinda cozy up to the preacher. And wham! Just like that! The old blackcoat would be tryin' to get into my petticoats quicker than the blink of an owl's eye."

Stroud, who'd been listening with raised eyebrows, roared. And Vivian joined in.

"Worked every time," she added. "Preachers are the biggest bunch of stiff-dicks I've ever known."

Stroud clutched his side and bellowed more boozy laughter.

"So I'd say no at first," she said after another sip of the rye. "Then me and Peter would plan a time and I'd let the old goat strip me naked, and just when he was about to taste the forbidden fruit, Peter'd come on the scene and threaten to expose God's very own servant unless he could get us a grubstake so's we could move on and leave the town in peace." She paused. "Baptists worked best."

"Baptists!" Stroud shrieked and slapped the table. "So how'd you get caught?"

"The last one was the first Lutheran we tried. And when Peter arrived on the scene all indignant, the son-of-a-bitch preacher pulled a thirty-two and shot Peter in the ass as he tried to run. Buck naked, I grabbed the gun away, but he came after me and it went off. Shot him in the side. I grabbed my dress, ran from the preacher's house, took his horse, and here I am. Saw in the papers that they both recovered. But the preacher was exiled and poor Peter went to jail," she finished, trying to look sad over Peter's demise. "That was almost a month ago."

"Well, ain't that somethin'!"

"Hope you don't think none the worse of me."

"Hell no, Lizzie. Might say I ride the wrong side of the law myself."

"Noooo."

"Yeah, you might say I'm in the stagecoach business."

"Really," Vivian said in a loud whisper. She clutched his leg. "That's exciting," she continued, her eyes fixed in a way that had Stroud drooling.

"Hey, Lizzie!" Chunk Frazer shouted from the other side of the saloon, breaking the spell she'd cast on the outlaw. "I ain't payin' you to be Stroud's personal barmaid. Get your ass up on your horse and ride. Drinks're backin' up."

"Oh, shit," Vivian said, grabbing his arm fondly. "I've gotta hustle. Let's have a drink tomorrow night after I'm off."

"Lizzie, you couldn't keep me away!"

THREE

The sun had been down for an hour and only a faint light prevailed in the western sky when Tallman rode into Red Rock astride a dappled gray. He was dusty and dirty and looked and smelled the part of a tough nut. As he loped past the business district toward the west end of the ramshackle town, he scratched at the two-day growth on his crusty face and wondered how Vivian was taking to the rat's nest they called Red Rock.

At once noticing the humdrum in the Silver Dollar, he halted his mount in front of the saloon, swung his leg over the gray, and planted his boots into the hardpan street. He adjusted his Model '72 Army Colt, felt for the .41 derringer he had in a small holster in the small of his back, and strolled into the bar, slapping his hat on his leg as he walked.

"Howdy, cowboy," a red-vested Chunk Frazer said from behind the bar. "What'll it be."

"Cold draught," he said, turning his back on the thick-necked barkeep.

The joint was in full swing even though it was early by more civilized standards. He noted several card games, hard cases swapping windy tales at the bar, and several solitary drunks well on their way to oblivion. The din of the crowd and the throbbing dissonance of the out-of-tune piano filled the wood-frame building. Then he heard her bawdy laugh.

Frazer clunked the mug on the crude bar. Tallman turned, fished a nickle out of his pocket, and slid it across the rough timber.

" 'Round here, mister," Frazer said, "beer's a dime."

Tallman eyed the barkeep, allowing a note of dissatisfaction. Then he shrugged and produced another coin. He hauled up the beer and swallowed half of it in the first gulp. Though the beer was warm and flat, it washed away the trail dust. He turned away from the bar again and took another draw on the mug. Out of the corner of his eye he saw Vivian acknowledge his presence with a raised eyebrow and widened eyes.

"Doc," Vivian said in a loud and playful voice, "tell us again about how you held off them redskins for two days without water or food."

Tallman nodded to let her know he got the message. Then he watched the man next to Vivian launch into a windy account of the gun battle.

His mind began to churn as he pondered the best

way to approach Stroud. Then it came to him when he took another sip of warm beer.

"Barkeep!" he shouted.

Frazer, who was in the process of serving another customer, spun on his heels. He was taken aback because people usually didn't yell at him.

"I ordered a *cold* beer," Tallman shouted again. "Bad enough you sellin' ten-cent beer. But this here shit ain't worth a goddamned nickle. Warm as fresh cow piss."

The room got quieter as Chunk Frazer walked along the bar toward Tallman, his menacing eyes glowing like hot coals.

Tallman saw that he'd figured the barkeep right. He'd enjoy a good skullbuster.

"Well, then, mister. You can take your business elsewhere," Frazer spat through gritted teeth. "Or—"

"Or, what?" Tallman interrupted, his jaw jutting defiantly.

"Or I'll swamp the floor with your carcass."

Tallman smiled at the thick-necked Frazer. He knew a down-and-dirty slugfest was the very thing to attract Doc Stroud's attention. While still smiling, he splashed the last third of his beer right in Frazer's face.

For a moment, surprise flickered in Frazer's eyes. Then he laughed out loud, planted his ham-sized hands on the rough-sawn bar top and vaulted. Tallman was waiting. He set himself and swung a hard-knuckled right to the side of Frazer's head as he was coming over the bar. The blow should have put the lard-bellied saloonkeeper down and out, but Frazer merely batted his eyes, shook his head, and swung a bruising left hook that mauled Tallman's ribs and sent him reeling backward. Like a lightning bolt, a Frazer right followed and grazed Tallman's ear. His hands down now, the saloonkeeper lumbered forward, confident of a quick end to the fight.

But Tallman snapped a rapid-fire right and left into Frazer's bent nose and slowed him momentarily. Shrugging at the blows, Frazer whistled an uppercut past his face. Seizing the opportunity, Tallman unloaded a solid left into the barman's soft belly. Air wooshed out in a sour wind and Frazer bent double. Tallman booted him in the crotch with all the power he had in his leg.

"Achhhh," Frazer grunted as he grabbed his balls.

Tallman relaxed his stance momentarily and glanced toward Stroud. The scarface had a bloodlust in his eyes.

Then Tallman's eyes widened as Frazer suddenly reared upright, shouted a bull-like bellow, and charged with a cocked fist. Tallman ducked aside as the saloonkeeper threw a haymaker that would have shattered a marble statue. The swing threw the barkeep off balance and Tallman unleashed another blow on the soft meat in Frazer's belly. The man's eyes went wide and he bent forward uttering strange noises, his mouth oozing a thin stream of stringy yellow slime. Amidst the dead silence of the room,

Tallman methodically hammered Frazer in the side of the head with three right hands.

The stone-headed Frazer stumbled with each blow but didn't fall. Tallman had never seen anyone take so much punishment in all his years of dealing out bare-knuckle justice.

Frazer attempted to charge again, but Tallman saw that he was on the edge. As the stooped-over hulk trundled forward, Tallman merely stepped aside and kicked the saloonkeeper in the side of the knee. A loud crack permeated the room and a grunt of pain burst from Frazer's lips. When Frazer reached for the broken knee, Tallman knuckled him right between the eyes. The stumbling form lurched sideways and fell onto a table, sending aloft a whirlwind of cards, glasses, whiskey bottles, and splintered tabletop. Groaning loudly and streaming blood from his nose, mouth, and a gaping cut over his left eye, Frazer rolled to one elbow in an attempt to get up. Tallman took two paces forward and kicked Frazer in the face. Teeth shattered and the saloonkeeper went face first into the rubble. He was out cold.

Tallman turned slowly, facing down the rest of the men in the saloon. "Any more pisswillies here who wanna take up the fat man's cause?"

No one spoke. Most bystanders refused to meet his eyes.

"We ought to buy that man a drink," Vivian whispered in Stroud's ear.

"Hey, there!" bawled Doc, at once following her suggestion.

Tallman spun, hands still balled in fists.

"Buy you a drink?" Stroud asked, as he motioned him back to the table.

"Who's askin'?"

"Name's Stroud. C'mon and take a load off your feet."

With a casual air, Tallman strolled through the rubble that had been a poker game and stepped over Frazer's limp form. He drew out a chair, reversed it, and straddled the seat with his lanky legs.

A flurry of activity centered over Frazer and someone said: "Get Doc Washington."

Stroud laughed. Then seeing that Tallman didn't get the joke, he explained. "Washington's the African who runs the livery. Fair horse doctor, but that's all."

Tallman smiled.

"Quickest hands I seen in a while," Stroud went on as he slid a glass toward Tallman and filled it with good rye. "What's your handle?"

"Dunn," Tallman said, making every effort to appear a loner. "Hoodoo Dunn."

"Sounds like it belongs on a wanted poster. You ridin' the owlhoot?"

Tallman remained quiet and sipped his whiskey.

"I mean, you don't look like no boot drummer," Doc added.

"Don't be bashful, Hoodoo," Vivian chimed in.

"Doc's Chairman of the Board of a stagecoach business."

Jake, Kirk, and Doc all laughed at the gaudy saloon girl.

"That's right Hoodoo," Stroud said, slurring his words. "Wells Fargo does all the work and we make the profits. If you get my meanin'?"

"Hell," Jake added. "Even Lizzie here's on the run."

"Ain't too many in Red Rock that ain't," the slender, black-haired Kirk busted in. "This here town ain't 'zactly your center of culture."

"Come on," Lizzie chided. "What's the law want with a good-lookin' man like Hoodoo Dunn?"

Tallman drained his glass and poured another.

"They hard on your trail?" Stroud asked.

"Mebbe," Tallman answered with a knowing grin.

"You'll be all right here," Kirk said with authority. "Law mostly stays away from here. Some son-of-a-bitch with a star'd be backshot before he walked half of Main Street."

Tallman drank with Vivian and the three outlaws for the next hour. He held his tongue for the most part, revealing only bits and pieces of a tale about small-time bank robbery. In the years he'd worked undercover for Pinkerton, he'd found that a closed mouth is one of the best character disguises a man can use. It lent an air of mystery to the part he was playing. And, since most people were blowhards, it allowed one to appear different if the situation required it.

After two hours of whiskey, gusty tales, and watching Doc and his two sidekicks dig at each other, Tallman realized he was hauling a good load of rye. Stroud had repeatedly hinted that they might use another hand, but he hadn't come right out and asked. Vivian had discreetly informed him during the well-oiled conversation that there was a third member of Stroud's gang who was on a rampage at the whorehouse on the edge of town. Finally it came.

"I like you, Hoodoo," Stroud said for the tenth time in the evening. "Took a likin' to you the minute I saw you handle Chunk Frazer. He's pure peckerwood. He's too stupid to know when he's well off. Now, me, I like doin' favors for fellers I respect. Law's easy and scarce 'round these parts, so I'm sure you'll be able to set up doin' banks like you was before." Stroud paused and gave Tallman a hard, squint-eyed look. "But keep in mind that we got a monopoly on the coaches, and anybody that fucks with our business gets his credit canceled, if you get my drift."

Tallman returned the look and nodded agreement.

"Unless, of course, you want to join us. I've took note that you ain't 'zactly buyin' too much whiskey tonight. Which means you ain't carrying gold."

"Jesus, Doc," Kirk butted in. "You ain't got the go-ahead on no more men."

Stroud eyed Kirk with a shut-up look.

"No mind," Tallman said to Kirk. "I ain't never worked a team and I guess I ain't about to start."

"Goddamnit," Stroud said, switching tactics abruptly. "Ain't too many men that turn down a split on twenty or thirty thousand in eagles and double eagles!"

Tallman straightened in his chair, raised his eyebrows, and held his glass of whiskey in midair.

"Easier haulin' some backwater bank. All gold. And we come up with coin every time or we don't ride," Stroud said.

Stroud fished a twenty-dollar gold piece from his pocket and slid it over under Tallman's eyes. Tallman eyed the double eagle greedily.

"Damnnn," he sighed. "I could use a grubstake."

"Doc," Jake said through his unkempt brown beard. "Pearl's gonna cut your nuts."

FOUR

Goddamn, Hoodoo, my head's about to come off," Stroud remarked as they loped single-file through a narrow pass. "Ain't sucked down that much likker in some months."

"Feels like I got a blacksmith workin' red-hot iron on the top o' mine," Tallman said truthfully, as he eyeballed the thousand-foot dropoff five feet to his right. He still didn't know the gray gelding that well. One bad step and it would be a long time before he reached bottom.

It was late afternoon, and the sun added to the misery of the five riders, all of whom had taken on a heavy cargo of popskull the night before. Except for the fuzz-faced kid, the riders kidded each other and laughed over already-exaggerated recollections of their exploits of the night before.

"Damn shame, Doc," Kirk went on. "I mean you missin' out on tastin' that Lizzie 'cause you was face-down asleep on the table."

The other three laughed. Doc was getting the worst of the jesting because he'd gotten so drunk he'd fallen asleep and no one had been able to wake him for five hours. For that, Vivian had been thankful.

"Don't fret none, Doc," Jake chimed in. "Pearl'll have ya pack her good when we get to camp."

Again they laughed at Doc.

That was the second time he'd heard the name Pearl. He gathered that she must be the gang's full-time cook and whore. He'd find that out soon enough.

Toward sundown the chatter died, and the grubby and weary riders topped another narrow pass and headed down a spiraling, rocky trail. In minutes Tallman saw their destination. A half hour away, an island of cool green lay at the bottom of a hidden valley. A narrow stream passed through a wide, rocky river bed that would have boiled with white water during the spring thaw. A thin ribbon of smoke arose from a clump of trees fifty feet from the stream. In the open, to the right of the trees, a dilapidated small gray barn, constructed of random-sized boards, leaned precariously toward the stream. A corral with half its rails missing was attached to the tilting barn. Some squatter's shattered dream.

It had been slow going on the narrow and rocky trail, but once they'd reached the grassy bottomland, Stroud spurred his horse into a fast trot and the others followed.

A quarter-mile out, Tallman saw the source of the

smoke. A crude, squat cabin lay in the grove of trees.

"I can't wait to see this," Kirk said to the bearded Jake as they dismounted.

"Do the horses," Stroud said to the kid after he dismounted.

Stroud and Tallman had to duck as they went through the six-foot door.

"Pearl," Stroud said, jerking his thumb over his shoulder toward Tallman. "Wan'cha ta meet Hoodoo Dunn."

Tallman leveled his eyes on the small, hawk-faced woman who sat in a crude chair behind a plank table. "Pleased to make the acquaintance, Pearl," Tallman said without a smile as he touched the brim of his dusty Stetson.

Pearl fixed her eyes in a devilish glare. The room got quiet. After a moment of silence, she looked toward Stroud.

"You-outta-your-fucking-mind-bringing-a-stranger-here!" she exploded. "What the hell's a matter with your lame ass."

"Wa . . . hell . . . Pearl . . . we can always use another good man," Stroud stammered, obviously defensive, and openly afraid of the small woman. "I . . . I've heard you—"

"You ain't heard shit," Pearl interrupted. "You stupid sonovabitch!"

Kirk snickered.

"Kirk! Shut up!" she shouted. "Jee-sus Christ. Damn you!" she said, turning back to Stroud. "You were drunk again. Weren't you!"

Tallman watched with fascination as Stroud stood with his head bowed and took her fusillade of insults. He was like a little kid taking a scolding for forgetting to feed the chickens. Kirk and Jake seemed to enjoy Stroud's discomfort, but it was obvious that they would have cowered under a similar attack. He figured he better step in to help Stroud.

"Ma'am," Tallman broke in softly. "It weren't exactly Doc's fault."

"Don't horn in, stranger," Pearl snapped back. "He screwed up bad and he knows it!"

"Only thing is," Tallman added pointedly. "I'm here."

The door swung open and the mean-eyed kid came in.

"Horses is put up!" he said.

"Yeah, you're here, all right," Pearl went on, disregarding the kid's entrance. "And you could disappear mighty goddamned fast."

Tallman at once sensed the danger. Everyone in the cabin froze. His eyes on Pearl, he backed away from the others and rested his hand on the butt of his Colt. He saw the blond-haired kid smiling for the first time since he'd met the gang of thieves.

"You want I should make this peckerface

disappear, Miss Pearl?" the kid asked as he also palmed the stag handles of his revolver.

"Well, now, Kriss," Pearl said, a sadistic smile painted on her sharp features. "Why don't you just do that."

Before she finished, the kid cleared leather and fired.

Instinctively, Tallman sidestepped, snatched the Colt from its well-oiled leather, and leveled his revolver. The gunhawk's first slug tugged at Tallman's shirtsleeve and thunked into the wall. Tallman fired as Stroud, Kirk, and Jake dove for the floor. His explosive slug caught the youngster square in the gut and doubled the wide-eyed kid over. Kriss fired his hogleg into the floor at his feet just as Tallman's second shot hit the retching kid in the top of the head. The force of the unique slug exploded on impact, sent a mist of gore across the room, and the dead stage robber hit the floor like a sack of corn. The prone corpse danced for an instant like a fresh-caught fish on a river bank, then stopped and leaked blood and urine.

Tallman shuffled sideways toward Pearl, eyeing the other three through the cloud of gunsmoke. When he reached her, he tipped her hat off with his gun barrel, grabbed a handful of hair, and pulled her head back as he pressed the Colt's muzzle hard to her temple. His anger welled.

"You sleazy bitch," he growled. "I ought to kill you and the rest of your goddamn gang."

"Jesus! . . . Easy does it, Hoodoo," Doc said as he hugged the gritty floorboards.

"Get up, bitch," Tallman said as he hauled the woman out of her chair by her hair. "Have a closer look," he continued to growl as he pushed her toward the body. "What do you see!" Tallman had never had to kill anyone as young as Kriss Kliegle, and the thought of it enraged him.

Pearl strained against Tallman's grip and turned to face him. "Looks good, don't he," she said, her face twisted in an erotic smile.

Tallman pushed her away. She stumbled over the body and fell.

"Doc, Kirk, Jake, and you, bitch," Tallman went on. "Get up! Unhitch them gunbelts real slow, and put the hardware on the table."

All four stage robbers complied. His rage was real, and he would have ended the Wells Fargo job right on the spot if any of the quartet had given him reason.

"Now, I'm goin' to ease outa here real slow," Tallman said, hoping for Doc to protest. "Anybody that follows gets to join the punk in Hell's fires."

"Damn, Hoodoo," Doc pleaded. "Cool your heels. Jake, you and Kirk get the kid outta here. Now, Hoodoo, holster that hogleg of yours and let's talk. You ain't leavin'."

"And the kid was fast with a gun," Pearl continued as she stared at the bloody form. "Real fast."

Kirk started to move toward the body after Doc's command.

"Hold it, Kirk," Tallman said, pointing his gun toward the outlaw.

Pearl turned to Tallman. "You ain't goin' nowhere, Hoodoo. We need another man, and looks to me like we ain't gonna find better. Kid was crazy anyhow. Couldn't be trusted. Always wantin' to shoot somebody."

Tallman didn't object as Pearl went matter-of-factly to the plank table and took her seat. "Do like Doc asked," she said toward Kirk and Jake. "Hoodoo, sit down. No hard feelings. Doc, get a bottle. We'll smoke the peace pipe."

"We'll talk," Tallman allowed. "But don't nobody put his gun on yet till I cool my jitters a bit."

"Throw them guns on the bunk," Pearl commanded Doc after he thumped a bottle of whiskey on the crude table. "Ain't no need for'em among friends."

Tallman sat down, still holding the Colt as it rested on the table.

Jake and Kirk, each with a foot, dragged the corpse across the floor, leaving a trail of gelled blood and brain matter. None of the four seemed the slightest bit affected by the carnage. Tallman had an iron stomach, but that moment he felt sick. There was something odd about this bunch. Tallman realized just then that, to a man, they had bent minds. They were black-hearted, stone-cold killers.

"Well, Hoodoo Dunn," Pearl went on. "You ever— Kirk," she interrupted herself as they went through the door and the remains of the kid's head thumped over the door jamb. "Get some river water and clean that shit off the wall and mop up the floor. You ever hit a stage, Dunn?"

FIVE

Tallman couldn't help smiling as he sat on the quiet river bank under the noon sun. Little Pearl Bowen treated the three outlaws like they were students in her school for retards. They hopped at her every command and withered when confronted with one of her outbursts of anger. Most amusing of all was the way she'd hauled Stroud to her little bedroom late the previous evening. Determined to keep one eye open throughout the night, he'd entertained himself by listening to a two-hour sex opera that was more humorous than erotic.

But, with a long pull on his cheroot, his smile vanished as he again thought of the kid who was dead and on his way to Hell before he'd grown hair on his face. The macabre picture of blood, bone shards, and pulpy brain matter was still etched clearly in his mind. He took a deep draw on the cigar and made a mental note to tell Aaron Wagner, his irascible

Chicago gunsmith, about the vaporization of the stage robber's head.

Wagner had developed the deadly round in his unique shop, and he would appreciate the report. He'd simply drilled the base of the slug, poured the cavity a third full of quicksilver, and sealed it. When the lead left the barrel, the liquid metal was plastered against the backside of the slug. On impact, it slammed forward and explosively sent chunked metal in every direction. He was pondering the fact that Wagner had explained, during his last visit, that he was working on a small spherical impact grenade, when Stroud interrupted his peaceful resting place.

"Got another one of them, Hoodoo?" Stroud asked as he approached and eyeballed the cigar.

Tallman fished another from his faded blue shirt pocket and tossed it upward to the scarfaced Stroud.

"Thanks, Hoodoo."

"Nice out here, ain't it, Doc?"

"I guess."

" 'Course, I wouldn't want to spend forever sittin' here."

"Nope," Stroud agreed as he sat in the river bank grass.

"Got any idea when we'll work?"

"Nope," Stroud answered as he fired up a sulphurhead on his bootheel. "But we'll get word when it's time," he went on as he exhausted a cloud of smoke. "Oughtta be soon enough."

"Hope so," Tallman said. "I got six silver dollars to my name."

"Gotta tell you, Hoodoo. I sure liked the way you cleaned up on Chunk Frazer and blowed the top of that punk's head off."

"They was askin' for it. Didn't give neither of 'em cause."

Stroud blew smoke rings.

"So we just sit and wait?" Tallman went on, trying to get back to the holdups. "Don't seem like much fun."

"Pearl will tell us when."

"Pearl! Harumph."

"She's boss, goddamnit."

"Seen that," Tallman grunted, squinting his eyes against the bright sun. "You start the gang or'd she?"

"Me. She used to be my steady woman. But once she got us a line on the shipments, she kinda took over."

"Got yourselves a Judas at Wells Fargo?" Tallman asked nonchalantly.

Stroud gave Tallman a wary look. "Once a secret's told it ain't a secret no more." He paused to blow smoke. "And don't never let Pearl hear such a question as that."

"What'll she do to me?" Tallman asked with a wide grin. "Haul me into that little room of hers and do me like she done you last night."

"You wiseass son-of-a-bitch," Stroud spat.

"Especially liked the time she sent you for some bacon grease so's you could poke her in the stink-hole."

Stroud jumped up, threw his half-smoked cigar on the ground and stomped it.

Tallman grabbed his side in laughter and rolled on the ground. *"Harder! Squeeze my tits! Bumfuck me! Harder! Harder!"* Tallman went on mimicking Pearl's raspy voice. *"Eat my snapper! Suck harder! Harder!"*

Stroud snatched his hat and threw it at Tallman. "Goddamn you, Hoodoo! Next time the laugh might be on you. Pearl likes variety, and I figure you're next. So we'll see who gets the last laugh."

"Me?" Tallman said as he held the laughter. "Naww."

"Let's just say you're in for a real treat!"

Then both men bellowed gut-wrenching laughter.

"Come on, Doc," Tallman said after the humor wore off. "Let's go into Red Rock and see if old Chunk Frazer's still alive. Mebbe I'll break his other knee."

"I don't know if Pearl—"

"Piss on Pearl," Tallman interrupted. "She ain't your mama."

Tears came with the renewed laughter, and Tallman forgot for the moment that it was his job to see Stroud dead.

Amidst laughter and a constant barrage of friendly jests, the pair saddled their horses and lit out for Red

Rock. Though it was only ten miles as the crow flies, the ride took three hours. On the way, Tallman avoided direct questions about the possibility of an insider at Wells Fargo. Instead, he worked hard at securing Stroud's trust and friendship. And he rambled on about Lizzie, the big-breasted saloon girl. He wanted to pair Doc up with Vivian and leave the interrogation to her, after he'd helped saturate Stroud with a full load of sourmash. It was, by now, obvious that the more the outlaw drank, the faster he talked.

The afternoon sun was pounding the earth as they finally emerged on the flatlands just north of town. It was a hundred in the shade.

"Let's start here," Tallman said as he hauled his horse around in front of the lopsided sign that advertised the Silver Dollar. "Take a look-see at Lizzie's tits."

Stroud followed without argument. His mood had fallen to a funk as he pondered Pearl's domination. He knew Hoodoo Dunn would never stand for it. His new gang member was the kind of hard case Stroud wanted to be, and Tallman's presence was Doc's unkind reminder of the fact that a small-tit hundred-pound woman ran his life.

A few idlers were tossing suds at the bar when they sauntered through the door. Chunk Frazer himself dealt the sole card game. As they passed the table, Tallman tipped his dusty Stetson at the crippled saloon owner. His left eye was black, his right eyebrow had been shaved and replaced with a line of knotted catgut stitches, and his leg was bound in a wooden splint with leather straps.

Vivian picked up on the pair as soon as they entered. By the time they got settled at a table against the wall, she arrived with three glasses and a bottle of Frazer's best whiskey.

"Howdy, Doc," she said as she sat down. "Figured you boys would be broke down for a week after all that whiskey the other night."

"Hell, Lizzie," Stroud said, his eyes glued to the creamy cleavage which welled over the front of her powder-blue dress. "We come to see you."

Tallman poured three glasses of whiskey. Stroud snatched his tumbler and tossed the whole shot in one stroke. Tallman relaxed. *That* was a good sign.

Before long, Stroud, egged on by Tallman, was crafting tall tales about his checkered past while Vivian pawed the outlaw fondly and kept his glass full. Once Tallman had to bite his tongue to keep from laughing as Vivian blatantly manipulated the windy fool.

Finally Stroud gave them the opportunity they were hoping for when he announced loudly that he was going to the outhouse. Tallman sighed as the outlaw stumbled off.

"What did you find out?" she asked, trying to fake the same smile and mood that had prevailed before Stroud left. "They the ones?"

"Looks like it. And get this! A little woman named Pearl Bowen runs the outfit."

"A woman!"

"Mean as a stepped-on rattlesnake. Wasn't there five minutes when she sicced that kid on me. I got lucky and he's dead," Tallman said, poking his finger through the hole in his blue shirt. "Fast gun. Poor aim."

"Oh, Ash," Vivian whispered, her eyes becoming wide with concern as she looked at the hole. "Be careful."

"I'm sure it's them," Tallman went on. "But I have nothing beyond the gang. I've tried Stroud a few times, but he clams up whenever I push. So I'm leaving that to you."

"He'll talk," Vivian said, a beguiling smile pasted on her painted face.

"I hope so," Tallman said. "We could put an end to this bunch right now. But something tells me the top dogs would easily find four more stoneheads just like Doc."

"Oh, Hoodoo!" Vivian whooped. "You rascal!"

Tallman took the warning and caught sight of Stroud out of the corner of his eye. "I think he knows something. Enough to keep the investigation alive," he whispered through closed teeth and a fake smile. "Work on it. And be careful. He's dumb but deadly."

"Well now Hoodoo, you *dooo* know how to tickle a lady's fancy!"

Tallman unleashed a loud horselaugh as Stroud sat down. If he knew *anything,* she'd know it too before the night was over.

"What's that?" Stroud asked.

"Old Hoodoo here was just tellin' me another of those tall tales," Vivian answered.

"Go on, Hoodoo," Stroud insisted, his lips thick with whiskey.

"Later, Doc. I'm gonna find me a card game and see if I can build on my six dollars. Hate like hell havin' you buy all the whiskey."

"Aw. Come on!"

"Mind's made up. You stay here and keep Lizzie in good company."

"Now that's a capital idea," she insisted, as she squeezed the outlaw's thigh under the table.

For over an hour, Vivian kept Stroud drinking, hoping to loosen his lips with her continuous flow of whiskey. She massaged his vanity with a steady stream of compliments on his wealth, good looks, and intelligence, almost choking every time she praised the latter. The theme of her slick dialogue was that Doc was so smart and so well connected that he might be able to get her back to doing something "more productive" than hustling drinks for Chunk Frazer. Twice she'd come right out and asked him who was running the stage-robbery operation, insisting each time that she would like to meet such people and better her station in life. But Stroud had clammed up each time, causing her to assume that he *did* know something.

"I just don't know what I'll do when *he* shows up at my door. So far, I've put him off with stories about how bad I'm havin' the curse this month," Vivian said of Frazer, as she, for the first time, touched the lump in Stroud's denims. "He's not my type . . . nothin' like you."

"I should be able to help somehow," he bragged, his eyes glassy, his speech thick. "I do got the connections."

"Oooo," Vivian groaned as she stroked the bulge more vigorously. "Let's go to my room where we can talk in private."

Stroud jumped at the suggestion, almost falling down as he got up. Once he had his balance, he followed her like a puppydog waiting for a bone. She had hoped that she would somehow escape without having to bed Stroud, but he'd been unwilling to reveal anything about his connections, so the most powerful of her interrogation techniques would, she'd decided, have to be employed. She was out to prove herself one of Pinkerton's best detectives, hoping to join the ranks of men like Ashley Tallman. And if that pursuit required a little rolling in the straw from time to time, she was willing and *very* able. As she walked to the back of the saloon with Stroud in tow, she mused that he might be good in bed. Even though he was a might soft in the head and a thief and killer to boot, he was not bad looking once you got past the mean eyes and the scar.

As soon as she'd closed the door to her small bare room, Doc pounced on her. With feverish abandon he pulled her bodice down with a sharp tug and greedily took a nipple in his mouth, sucking, slurping, and nipping.

"Oooo, Doc. That feels good. Ahh." She wasn't being dishonest. "But let's go . . . Ahhh . . . Doc, let's go real slow. That's the way I like it," she said as she lifted his head away from her bare breasts. "Slow and easy."

Stroud backed away and began to fumble with his gunbelt and trouser buttons. His glazed eyes and labored breathing signaled Vivian that he was in no mood for tender and lingering sex. Within seconds he'd shed his clothing in a heap and had flopped on the rickety wooden-frame bed.

"Goddamn, Lizzie," he grunted as he took his stiff cock in his hand. "Drop them rags and sit on this."

Ignoring his urgent command, she disrobed slowly and erotically, all the while pumping the tightly wound outlaw on his connections. "I've simply gotta get something going for myself," she went on as she rolled a stocking slowly down her long shapely leg. "And I know you're hooked into the big-time somehow, Doc. I mean, everybody talks about how you and your boys only hit the right stagecoaches."

"They do," he said as he released the hold on his meat. "I ain't heard that."

"Why Doc, nobody's got the guts to say anything to your face," she said as she threw the stocking aside and put her other foot on the bed, giving Stroud a view of the reward which lay just under sheer silk panties. "A girl's got to take care of herself. And that's all I'm tryin' to do. You gotta help me, Doc."

"Goddamn, Lizzie," Stroud grunted. His speech was thicker and his eyes looked out of focus. "Get them skivvies off."

"I've got to get out of here, Doc," she went on. "And you're my only chance." With that she lowered the panties, revealing a triangle of auburn hair and the gateway to her womanhood. "You simply have to help, Doc," she pleaded as she lay down next to the drunken outlaw. "Please."

Without muttering a sound, he grabbed her pubic mound, jabbed a finger into her moist opening, and again latched on to an erect nipple with his wet mouth.

"Oh, Doc," she groaned, "that feels good."

She *was* enjoying his rough and greedy approach, taken, as always, by the power of her sex. When men reached the point where they lost control, she likewise focused her mind on that ultimate moment when, like magic, waves of pleasure would sap all her tension and leave her with several moments of perfect bliss.

"Oh, Doc," she whispered, aroused by the loud sucking and the rough finger.

Then she cupped his sac and began to gently massage the nuggets within. "Please help me, Doc," she went on. "You know I'll approach your people on the sly so they'll never suspect anything. They'll never know you told," she continued as she began to finger the tip of his swollen cock.

"Ahhh, Lizzie," Stroud said after he stopped his sucking and nipping. "Jesus, I don't know."

"Come on, Doc," she insisted as she began to pump his shaft while holding it snugly. "Just a name. Just a name and I'll do the rest."

"Sherm Jarrott," Stroud blurted, his words run together with booze. "Owns a gambling joint in Tucson."

"Thanks, Doc," she whispered in his ear as she stroked harder. "You've saved my life."

Stroud lurched to his side and grabbed her shoulder. In one violent movement he pulled her on top. "Now ride, goddamnit!" His drunken words were almost incomprehensible. "Sit on it!"

Vivian got to her knees and reached between her legs for his throbbing cock. She was ready, even anxious. She held the stiff meat and stroked the length of her opening with the head of his rod until it was dripping with her juices. Stroud had a distant look in his glassy eyes when she lowered herself on the blue-veined shaft. Then like a lamp run dry, he flickered and went out. He breathed deeply and his meat went soft, flopping away from her moist curls.

SIX

Vivian was contemplating their good luck as the stagecoach rocked and rattled over the rutted Tucson Road. With a minimum of effort, Tallman had infiltrated the gang and she'd been able to pry a name from Stroud. In their short meeting after Stroud had passed out, they both had agreed that Jarrott must have had something to do with the stage robberies. The Wells Fargo district office was in Tucson, and a bum like Stroud wouldn't otherwise have known a casino owner in Tucson.

In spite of the heat and the bug-eyed farm-implement wholesaler who'd been bending her ear and eyeing her body, she was jubilant. But building a case that would make it through the courts was harder than she imagined, especially when high-level political skulduggery was involved. She'd find that out, soon enough.

As the team strained on a winding grade, the image of Stroud's untimely sleep brought a smile to her tastefully made-up face. It had been two days since the scarfaced outlaw had gone down in a whiskey haze. For a moment she'd been angry as she held the shriveled penis. Then, at the next instant, she'd been struck silly with the scene. The boastful, mean-eyed, scarfaced outlaw . . . with a limp pecker.

Even as she'd gotten dressed, the nude stage robber lay as still as a corpse. Anxious to get the information to Tallman, she had worked the floor for another half hour before informing Chunk Frazer that she was taking fifteen for a breath of fresh air. Tallman had noted her departure and begged out of his poker game for a trip to the outhouse.

Minutes later, they had met in the shadows of the alley and decided that she should employ her skills as a card slick and pose as a high-class lady gambler, in an effort to get close to this Sherm Jarrott, while he stayed with Pearl Bowen and her three mutts.

"Where will you be staying in Tucson?" the farm-equipment drummer asked, his words jolting her to the present, his eyes obviously flickering with images of nude flesh.

"I don't know," Vivian said to the only other passenger, her words as crisp and refined as the dark-blue dress she was wearing. "What hotel do you recommend? I usually like to have the best."

"The Governor," he said enthusiastically. "It's the best in Tucson. Usually stay there myself," he lied.

Vivian nodded with indifference toward the sweaty, round-faced man, who wore a suit which was obviously more expensive than his earnings would justify. He continued to talk as she half-listened and looked at the desolate country that passed beyond the coach window.

The drummer continued to babble as if she were hanging on his every word while she wondered how this portly blabbermouth could sell a two-cent cup of water to a millionaire stranded in the desert.

When they finally lurched to a stop in front of Wells Fargo's Tucson depot, her shoulders sagged momentarily in an expression of relief. If the short, chubby drummer's yackety-yack had gone on any longer she would have lost her composure.

As she waited on the boardwalk for the driver and the guard to fetch her bag, the peddlar asked her to dinner, his voice ringing with phony salesman self-confidence.

"Well . . . dinner . . . maybe," Vivian said as she faked a seductive voice. "But first tell me what we'll do after dinner."

"Well, I . . . d-don't," he stammered as his face reddened.

"I'm really quite worried that you might not be able to find your little pee-wee in all that lard," she bellowed as she stared right at his crotch.

The two coachmen howled with laughter as the salesman waddled off, suffering a case of terminal humiliation.

When the humor died, the driver gave her directions to the Governor and confirmed that it was the best hotel in town. Then she nodded toward an eager bag boy who had a big smile, which was a remnant of her spicy putdown of the drummer.

After three blocks of commercial buildings with colorful false fronts, they came to a sturdy frame building that was painted a pleasing light powder gray and trimmed in a dark blue. A deep-red sign, with routed edges and routed lettering inlaid with gold leaf, stated regally: *The Governor Hotel.*

"Here you are, young man," she said to the boy as she dropped a half-dollar into the lad's small, hungry hand. "And before you go, would you please tell me where I might find Mr. Sherm Jarrott's casino?"

Once in her room, Vivian put the contents of her two bags either in a fine handcrafted dresser or on the silk-padded hangers in the closet. She was glad to have retrieved her good things from the stage depot at Eloy. Truth be known, she didn't enjoy herself as much when she had to play the part of a floozy, mainly because she disliked cheap clothing. She slumped in the overstuffed wingback chair, suddenly feeling tired as she contemplated the whirlwind activity of the last two days.

Later in the same evening that had seen Stroud's drunken failure in bed, Frazer had insisted on taking a piece of her flesh for himself. Overjoyed with a convenient reason to bolt town, she'd slapped Frazer on his stitched eye and fled to her room. Frazer, purple with anger, had limped after her, but the hard case named Hoodoo Dunn had intercepted the splint-legged tree-stump. "Don't think Doc Stroud would appreciate you buttin' in," he'd growled. "I know I don't!"

Thankful for Tallman's intervention, she had packed her single ragged carpetbag as Stroud snored without skipping a beat. After spending the rest of the night in the Red Rock stage depot, she'd taken the eight o'clock to Eloy, where she'd left her good things on the trip in from Santa Fe. After one day to reorganize, she'd spent the morning with the flap-jawed drummer. And that had brought her to her momentary exhaustion. Recalling that she'd noticed an elegant-looking ladies' bath at the end of the hallway, she decided on a hot soaking in the tub.

It was four in the afternoon by the time she'd cleaned up and decked herself out as she might have for any evening out in Chicago. As she applied temperate makeup, she kept reminding herself to drop the slang and purposeful abuse of the English language that she'd used in Red Rock.

Satisfied with her looks, she left the second-floor room and came down the spiral mahogany stairs into the expensively appointed lobby.

"Good afternoon, Miss Duncan," the clerk said pleasantly when she passed the front desk.

"Good afternoon," she replied after taking several steps before recognizing her own name. "You must forgive me," she went on as she stopped and turned. "My mind is in another place."

As she sauntered along the boardwalk, she imagined that Tucson was a town with a future. Though still a speck on the savage land, the Arizona territorial capital was alive with commerce. People strode to and fro, their eyes set on some distant goal. Wagons bulging with freight rumbled in the hardpan streets, and the stores were well stocked and bustling with customers.

After crossing four streets, she turned left at Abelson's Dry Goods and went only a short distance into Tucson's "amusements" district before she saw the Buena Suerte on the right. The bag boy's directions had been exact. No doubt he'd given them many times before.

Vivian opened the heavy casino doors, which were decorated with stained-glass windows, one an artistic replica of the jack of spades, the other, the ace of hearts. Just as she set foot in the door, a piano, a five-string banjo, and a bass fiddle came to life as if to announce her entrance. Momentarily taken aback by the random occurrence, she stopped at the door and looked about the large room. As far as small-town Western gaming joints went, Sherm Jarrott's Buena Suerte was among the top twenty percent.

When she noticed eyes focusing on her entrance, she strode toward the bar as if she belonged.

"Mr. Jarrott in?" she asked.

"He's in his office, but he don't wanna be bothered," the barkeep said as he polished glasses.

"Where is his office?" she insisted, her voice full of authority.

"Up there," the bartender said in a flat voice as he nodded toward the balcony overlooking the floor, which was already teeming with card games, scantily clothed drink hustlers, whirring roulette wheels, and highly animated and boisterous dice throwers.

"He'll see me," she said firmly. "It's personal."

"I don't know, lady."

"Trust me," she said, stabbing him with her mellow voice and determined smile.

With a host of eyes following, she made her way across the room toward the stairs that led to the balcony. Once at the top, she found the door marked with a brass plate: OFFICE.

"What!" a peevish voice said from behind the door.

She opened the door and took several steps into the room with practiced and bold determination. It always worked.

"Yes?" the man asked from his leather chair, his hands planted on the polished mahogany desk top.

"Susanna Duncan," she said as she extended her hand and glued her eyes on the bridge of his nose.

"What can I do for you?" the man asked, his voice flat.

"It's simple, Mr. Jarrott," Vivian said. "I think I'll be working for you once you give me the opportunity to prove to you that I can put money in your pocket."

"Oh!"

"So far, I've never known a casino owner to turn down a blackjack dealer who could keep the house ahead . . . always."

"Do we have some mutual friend, Miss Duncan?"

"No," she said. "I just asked around and soon determined that I'd see you first."

Jarrott stared back through his wire-rimmed glasses. Though he was in his middle forties, he looked younger, even considering the thinning brown hair. His face was tanned and a thick red-brown mustache and bushy dark eyebrows accented his angular jaw. He was a good-looking man by any standards.

"Sit down . . . please, Miss Duncan," he said, closing the black-leather ledger on his desk. Once he had cleaned the desk top, he produced a deck of cards, which was wrapped in paper and sealed with the manufacturer's stamp. With no talk, he slid the package toward his uninvited visitor. His face revealed that he had seen a lot of self-proclaimed card artists, and that he guessed that she was just another inept dreamer.

Vivian scooted forward on her chair and accepted

the cards. After she deftly broke the seal, the deck fell into her right hand and she fanned them on the table in one fast stroke, which left the cards perfectly spaced so as to reveal the upper-left corner of each. She then took the jokers between her fingertip and thumbnail and flipped the fifty-two pasteboards face down, making the deck act like a giant inchworm taking a quick step. She dropped the jokers to one side and collected the cards into a perfect stack with another snap of her agile hand as Jarrott's eyes widened slightly.

Vivian kept her stare fixed on Jarrott's eyes while she shuffled five times. Jarrott saw her organizing the deck, but admitted to himself that few if any would be able to catch the moves. Then she began dealing, pulling seconds and bottoms so expertly that he missed most of her work. In less than three seconds eight cards lay on the table, four aces up. Then she turned the bottom cards: ten of hearts, king of diamonds, jack of clubs, and jack of spades.

"Blackjack," she said, faking surprise in her voice.

Then, with equal skill and speed, she dealt four more hands with two up. As Jarrott watched, Vivian turned the bottom cards.

Jarrott nodded, aware of her point.

"You agree, Mr. Jarrott, that the cards compel the player to take another?"

He nodded again.

Then she snatched four more cards, each of which put the hands over twenty-one.

"Would you like me to tell you which twenty-eight cards I have left and the odds in favor of and against the house based on any hand you might make out of any three of the twenty-four cards down?" she said with a smile that would disarm any man. "Or should I go on?"

"Well, Miss Duncan," Jarrott responded after clearing his throat. "I'd say I'm having a lucky day. I'm glad I was first on your list. Hate like hell to have you working for one of my competitors."

"I don't want a wage," she said. "Fifty-fifty split on the table's take. I guarantee you that no one will be the wiser. I'm well aware that greed can easily kill the goose that lays the golden eggs."

"I don't doubt your understanding of the game," Jarrott said as he removed the silver-rimmed glasses and set them on the closed ledger. "But something does bother me. I wonder if you might explain why you're in Tucson. It's obvious that a lady of your skills and, I might add, beauty, could work better gaming houses than the Buena Suerte."

"You are very observant, Mr. Jarrott," she agreed, her eyes beaming sexual energy. "But . . ."

"Sherm," Jarrott interrupted.

"Sherm . . . Well, you might say I was a victim of circumstances."

"How so?"

She explained that she had worked a very profitable casino on the Barbary Coast. For over a year, she'd run the biggest and the most popular table for the owner, who, for some reason unknown to her, fell out of grace with the crooked San Francisco political structure. His rivals had hired an expert and sent the card shark and two undercover lawdogs to her table. They'd accused her of numerous violations of the local laws. Once caught, she explained to Jarrott, she had faked an illness and escaped the hospital in only a nightgown.

"A friend got me on a ship for Puerto San Carlos, halfway down Baja," Vivian went on. "That was over a month ago. My boss wasn't as lucky. I heard he'd been robbed and had his throat cut in the process. You don't fight politicians and their silver-starred henchmen for too long and get away with it. At least, that's been my experience."

"I see," Jarrott said as he knuckled his mustache. A wide smile came to his face. "Politics will not be a problem in Tucson," he bragged, already working on having more of Susanna Duncan than her mastery of the pasteboards. "In fact, you're welcome to start now, if you wish."

"Lead the way," she said. "I need to put a little weight in my purse."

"And how about a late dinner or early breakfast? Your choice."

"I'd love it," she said honestly, as she again contemplated the speed of her progress. "Dinner sounds fine."

Jarrott spent the next half hour explaining the details of his gambling operation, including his scheme for rewarding political hacks with net winnings whenever he signaled her to do so. Down on the floor, he introduced her to the floor manager, Obie Stallybrass, the other dealers, the six bar girls, and the two bartenders.

As she followed Jarrott about the floor, Vivian was amused, as she often was, at how easily a person could take a slice of the world with only the right mix of common wisdom, a bold manner, and self-confidence. It was one of the things that continued to amaze her after all her years as a bunco artist and now, still as a Pinkerton operative. It was so easy, she mused, but most accepted their miserable stations and wasted a lifetime blaming every*one* and every*thing* for their broken dreams. From her vantage point, this was one of life's imponderables.

An hour and a half after she'd poked through the stained-glass doors, she was dealing to three respectable types who were decked out in suits, clean stiff collars, and polished boots.

As the evening advanced, store owners, miners, cowhands on the drift, itinerant peddlers, and a host of suspicious-looking characters with no apparent purpose or profession all tested their skills against her version of that cruel mistress, Lady Luck. Some won. Others lost. And she was hauling in plenty, hoping to keep Jarrott happy.

As the beer and whiskey consumption went up, so did the noise. By eleven, the trio of red-vested musicians could barely overcome the din of laughter, the hoots of winners and, more often, the muffled curses that came as gold and silver coin slid across the green felt into the hands of the house.

In a few short hours, Vivian had fallen into her role. With the exception of the name, there was really little difference between Susanna Duncan and Vivian Valentine. The crafty blackjack dealer and the undercover Pinkerton were *really* the same woman.

She pondered that bit of reality as she dealt to one drunken mark with three crooked piles of silver dollars, and to two newcomers, one fat and one slender and tall. She baited the drunk and the tall newcomer with winnings and took from the fat man with stupid eyes.

"Well, Oscar," the tall new player said. "If my luck's as strong as this lady is on looks, I'll own Jarrott's place before sunup."

"I do declare, you gentlemen sure know how to talk to a lady."

"Old Abelson here's got a smooth tongue, miss. But don't get near his dry-goods emporium or he'll have your month's wages before you've walked one aisle."

Vivian dealt twenty-one for Abelson and busted the drunk and the fat man called Oscar.

"Damn," the hog-jowled gambler said, as he tugged at his collar and loosened his shoestring tie. "Right off to a shitbucket start."

Vivian gave him a fake sheepish look.

"You've got your nerve, Oscar. Tellin' this lady

that I'd take her wages," Abelson said. "You and your cronies down at the courthouse got a line of bullshit a mile long. And when you take somebody's money, they don't get nothin' for it but more laws and more bureaucrats."

Oscar swooped winnings after he'd doubled up. Vivian had gathered that he was a political hack of some sort and she figured to hype him up for a big kill.

"You in politics?" she asked the bulbous player.

"Mayor Oscar Westfall," he said proudly as he jammed a cigar as big as an ax handle into the corner of his chubby pink lips. "Mayor of the fair city of Tucson."

"Well, sir, I'm proud to make your acquaintance," Vivian lied, her eyes suggesting that she might eat him alive in the goose down. "I'm new in town. Got in only this morning, and Mr. Jarrott was kind enough to give me employment."

Having always thought of politicians as the most dishonorable of all charlatans, she proceeded to rob the mayor of his silver as fast as he laid it on the felt. At the same time, she returned some of Abelson's taxes. At least, she thought to herself as she skillfully raked in the mayor's money, most crooks she'd known made no pretense about being anything *but* crooks. But politicians, she'd observed, had, without exception, veiled their skulduggery and vain deeds in a cloak of self-righteousness.

She was just about to finish off Westfall's purse when Jarrott approached.

The casino owner slapped the mayor on the back and shook Abelson's hand.

"Howdy, Sherm," Westfall grunted as a one-inch chunk of cigar ash fell unnoticed into his lap. "See you got yourself a new dealer."

"And a mighty pretty one," Abelson added. "Bringing me a fine streak of luck too."

"Wish I could say the same," the mayor wheezed through a cloud of acrid smoke.

"Stick with it, Oscar. Maybe your luck will turn," Jarrott said as he looked toward Vivian and tugged on his earlobe. "Your credit is always good in the Buena Suerte."

Vivian saw the signal and begrudgingly but skillfully reversed the flow of coin to Westfall's favor. As Jarrott walked off, she smiled, recalling Jarrott's statement: *Politics will not be a problem in Tucson.*

She knew better. Politics was always a problem . . . everywhere.

SEVEN

Dogshit!" Pearl grunted after throwing her cards on the scattered coins in the middle of the table. "You got a four-leaf clover up your ass, Jake."

"'Bout time, Pearl. You've damn near run me dry," Jake said through his beard. Then, after a pause, he added: "Run me dry of coin, that is."

Doc and Kirk laughed aloud at Jake's reference to his raucous night in bed with Pearl.

"Shut up, you peckerheads," Pearl spat. "Jake! Deal! And pour me another whiskey, Hoodoo!"

"Yes'm," Tallman chided, faking a slave-to-master tone as he poured the last of a bottle into her glass. "Anything you want, Mizz Pearl."

Doc and Kirk snickered at Tallman's wiseass response as Pearl glared at the newest member while she picked up her cards.

Though Tallman was playing along, he was quickly growing tired of cards, whiskey, and childish verbal grab-ass. Were it not for the odd amusement he got out of Pearl's domination of Doc, Jake, and Kirk, the previous three days would have seemed endless.

Somehow, this woman had turned a small gang of nitwits into deadly, big-stakes stagecoach robbers. She was obviously very intelligent, and Tallman sensed a formal education, even though she did her best to look and act like the flintheaded wife of a squatter. Her mouth was foul, but her willingness to open her legs for her troopers provided Tallman with the ultimate amusement.

"That's better, Jake," Pearl said, looking at her cards. "Keep 'em comin' like that and I might let you get that beard wet again tonight."

Jake raised his eyebrows while Tallman, Doc, and Kirk roared again with whiskey-saturated laughter.

"You gonna have Jake feed at the old honey-pot, Pearl?" Tallman asked after he looked at his cards. Though he felt like a fool playing games with this strange quartet, he wanted Pearl to think she had another lamebrained hard case to add to her collection.

"Keep it up, Hoodoo, and I'll have you eatin' honey."

"Goddamn, Pearl!" Doc shouted. "Think me and Kirk could watch?"

"For chrissake, play poker," Jake groaned as he slid five silver dollars to the center of the table.

As the betting began to develop, the hooting and laughter subsided. Pearl had taken only one card, while Doc stood firm and the others had taken three each. Tallman had drawn a six of diamonds, a nine of clubs, and a two of spades to a pair of fours. "I'm goin' to open another bottle," Tallman said as he chucked his cards. "If I stay in this rip, I'll be playin' for my spurs before long."

As he snatched a new bottle of cheap rye off the shelf, he laughed to himself. With only the most basic moves, Vivian could have cleaned Pearl and her soft-headed troopers in two hours. In all his years, he'd never seen anything like her mastery of the pasteboards. He truly felt sorry for Tucson's gamblers.

After he squeaked the cork free, he took a small pull on the bottle and again mused on Pearl's odd nature. Aside from her plain, hawkish features, her body was well above average. He'd guessed her to be mid-thirties. Her shirt was undone at the top and he could see two small mounds that were topped with jutting nipples.

As he stood there holding the bottle, he again wondered how Vivian was doing. He could never quite shed his concern for her. He'd talked her into the business and, though he'd sworn to himself he wouldn't, he felt responsible for her safety. If you made one slip when you were dealing with big money and black-hearted beasts like those at the table in front of him, you got your final reward, six feet of dirt.

"Hoodoo," Pearl commanded. "You gonna stand there and hold that bottle all goddamn day? Bring that corn over here, for chrissake!"

"Goddamn, Pearl," Tallman said as he walked around the worn plank table. "Where do you put all the firewater? Ain't never seen a lady drink so much as you!"

"Lady!" Kirk sighed. "Well now. Looks like ol' Hoodoo's pitchin' woo at Pearl."

"Shut up, shitbreath!" Pearl said with raised eyebrows and tight lips. "Or you ain't gonna dip that little mule of yours for a month of Sundays."

Kirk's face went red and he looked like a kid who'd been caught jerking off in the schoolyard. While Kirk bled, the other four jabbed and howled. Suddenly, the fit of tearful laughter died as the sound of a single rider penetrated the cabin. Pearl's loudmouthed jesting stopped instantly and she popped out of her chair, her mood at once as serious as a preacher's at graveside.

"All right you boneheads, find somethin' to do," Pearl ordered. "Kirk, Jake, and Hoodoo! Clear out!"

"Let's go on down to the stream," Kirk suggested as they shuffled out the cabin door together. "I'm gonna take me a bath and soak some of this whiskey out of my head. Looks like we'll be workin' in a day or two."

"Messenger?" Tallman asked Kirk as he looked over the rider and his horse, noting every detail.

"Yeah," Kirk said under his breath as if the obvious was some big secret.

"Who the hell is he?"

"Don't know, Hoodoo," Kirk said. "And I ain't gonna stick my nose in."

"And you'd be smart to do the same," Jake added as he stroked his beard. "Don't let all Pearl's bullshit and fuck talk fool you none. She ain't as dumb as she looks, and she gets real upset when anybody butts in on the details of her operation. Piss her off and she could cut your fuckin' balls off and eat 'em raw while you watched . . . and that's gospel."

"Jake's got it straight," Kirk added. "Woman's got turpentine for blood."

"Mebbe so," Tallman said, slightly taken aback by the serious tone of their warnings. "But," he went on, hoping to change the subject, "I'd like to see if she's all that cold when she's got a sausage stuck between them little legs o' hers."

"You'll find out soon enough," Kirk said as they reached the stream. Then the two outlaws howled in harmony and ran into the water fully clothed.

After less than five minutes, the rider departed in a cloud of dust. Tallman would have given a pound of gold to have a way to tail the messenger, but, given Pearl's nature, he knew no excuse would permit his departure. So he soaked up the afternoon sun and wished that he hadn't had so much of the bad whiskey. For three hours, the trio jawed and smoked. Tallman had tried to get more detail from the pair of robbers, but it had soon become obvious that they knew very little. He had learned one thing, though.

Pearl was more dangerous than a cornered mama grizzly. Kirk and Jake had recounted several of their previous holdups and revealed that Pearl commanded the operation and that she'd personally killed the Wells Fargo employees.

"Get your asses up here!" Stroud hollered from the cabin, breaking the boredom of the three-hour wait. "We're goin' to work."

"Hot damn," Jake said as he got up. "My stash o' gold's just about shit the bed."

"What do you figure we'll get?" Tallman asked as they walked up the incline.

"Don't know, Hoodoo!" Jake said, his voice brimming with enthusiasm. "Could be two thousand! Or more! Usually is!"

When they walked in the door, Pearl and Doc were hunched over a dog-eared map. "Get your butts over here," she growled without looking up. "Vacation's over."

"Got somethin' big for us, Pearl?" Jake went on, glowing like a kid at a birthday party.

"Over twenty thousand. Gold coin. No banknotes. And maybe something bigger a week from now."

"Ain't that somethin', Pearl," Tallman said quietly as he laid a line of tobacco on a cigarette paper. "Your Judas even tells you how much."

The room got quiet as Pearl slowly looked up from her map and scowled at Tallman through pursed lips and narrowed eyes. "Hoodoo, get your ass over here and don't worry none about nothin' but what I tell you to worry about."

"Hell, Pearl! No need to git sore," Tallman whined as he put a flaming sulphurhead to his freshly rolled cigarette. "Just strikes my fancy the way you got this all worked out. Slicker than babyshit for sure."

"Stage leaves Tucson tomorrow morning at seven," she continued, turning back to the wrinkled map and ignoring Tallman. "We're going to hit it in Picacho Pass. They got about forty miles to do before the pass, so I want us there no later than eight-thirty. That should give us plenty of time."

Tallman smoked and took in every detail of the operation even though he appeared indifferent. He had been especially interested in her mention of another job within the week. A rough outline of a plan to put the gang out of business began to develop in his mind.

"Where they got it hid this time?" Jake asked.

"Floorboards," Doc responded quickly. "We'll have to bring a wreckin' bar."

"How much firepower they bringin'?" Tallman asked.

"One man riding shotgun," Pearl said. "Word is, he's a tough nut, so keep your eyes on him."

"Just like before, Pearl?" Kirk asked.

"Right. Only Hoodoo takes the kid's place," Pearl said, looking at Tallman with strange eyes. Then she paused. "Fucking shame," she finally sighed. "Hurts every time I think of it."

As Pearl went on to explain every detail of her plan, Tallman was further taken with her mind for strategy and detail. Like Kirk said, she was not as dumb as she made herself out to be. Obviously a woman who'd discarded all social convention and become the ultimate scofflaw, Tallman wondered several times what she would be like under the sheets. And as she went over the lay of the land around Picacho Pass, he also pondered on how a person could get so far out of step with the rest of the world.

The planning and Pearl's tiring rehearsals went well into the evening. Tallman listened halfheartedly after a while, and he began to entertain disjointed thoughts about Vivian's progress, the identity of the inside man at Wells Fargo, and Pearl's outrageous behavior. But mostly he worried about his partner in Tucson. This was only their second case, and, although she'd worked like an old hand during the Southern Pacific Railroad operation, they'd dealt mostly with con men and charlatans. Though dangerous, they were not as ruthless and bent as this gang of cold-blooded killers, who'd taken pleasure in cutting up a sixty-year-old boot drummer for a sliver dollar. If the men at the other end of this operation were half as bad as Pearl's bunch, Tallman thought to himself, Vivian could be in over her head.

EIGHT

Mayor Westfall hauled in a pile of silver dollars as Vivian retrieved the cards. Out of the corner of her eye, she saw the dapper Jarrott give her a wink of approval and a thin-lipped smile. Regardless of Jarrott's transgressions, Vivian had discovered that she could not dislike the man. And today, the Buena Suerte owner looked especially sharp in a dark-blue conservative plaid. This was only their third night, and she'd already decided that she liked him enough to enjoy herself in the event she had to use her ultimate weapons to loosen his tongue. So far, he'd been the perfect gentleman. But she suspected that his temperate behavior was simply a part of *his* approach to the grand game of pursuit and conquest.

As she fingered another winning hand for the lard-assed mayor, she reasoned that it could be a whole lot worse. In her days as a con artist, she'd played up to some pretty disgusting characters, many of whom made Mayor Westfall look like a saint.

"Go again," Westfall said to Vivian after he slid two eagles forward on the felt and wiped the sweat from his fat brow. "I can feel the luck in my bones."

"Damned if you ain't had it, Mayor," sighed the hotel owner to his right. "I haven't won a goddamned nickel."

"Hell, Henry. You can afford it," Westfall wheezed as he mopped more sweat from his pink face. "The rates you charge!"

"Bets, gentlemen?" Vivian asked.

"Now, Mayor! What would you ever do without my hotel?" Henry said as he placed money next to his cards. "You'd have no place to take your young lady friends. I mean, Minnie don't let you take them home, does she?"

With that, the onlookers and the other three at the table erupted in a fit of teary-eyed laughter. It was obvious that Mayor Westfall was often the focus of casino buffoonery. In Tucson it was like it was in most places. The local politicians were either crafty charlatans or self-serving bunglers who were unknowingly used by the behind-the-scenes power brokers. Westfall was in the latter category.

"And you a deacon of the church and all," one of the bystanders chimed in. "Praise the Lord!"

Westfall grumbled a curse and gave Vivian a sheepish grin.

"Got an eye for the ladies, Mayor?" Vivian asked with sultry eyes as she pitched the cards.

"These loudmouths," he grunted.

"Oops," Vivian said as she flipped a queen of diamonds on Westfall's upturned two of spades and nine of hearts. "Guess Lady Luck's on break."

Jarrott had explained to her that she was to keep Westfall up sixty or seventy dollars a week on average. In the past hours she'd been building him up for the sting. He had more than three hundred dollars in front of him. Now she would assist the others in slashing Westfall into a state of ill humor.

Jarrott saw what was happening and chuckled out loud as he hoisted a cold, frothy mug of beer and toasted Vivian from afar. Vivian allowed a sly smile for the casino owner and scooped up more of Westfall's winnings, just as the three-piece band struck a lively tune, as if to celebrate the happy mood that now permeated the air. Onlookers and the others at the table jabbed and snickered as Westfall's pile of coins diminished with every hand. Elsewhere in the crowded room, whiskey, beer, and money were flowing like white water in a rain-swollen stream.

Just as she scooped Westfall for the fifth time, two ominous characters bulled their way through the colorful glass doors. Then she saw Jarrott thump his mug on the polished bar and scamper toward the taller of the two. While dealing, she watched carefully as Jarrott pumped the man's hand and slapped his back, paying no attention to the shorter man, who had the eyes of the devil and the nose of a rundown prizefighter.

After a brief ceremony, the three men scurried

toward the stairs. As they hurried by the blackjack table, Vivian noticed that Westfall paused, raised an eyebrow, and shook his moist pink jowls. He obviously knew the visitors. But he seemed to take no special pleasure in that fact.

"Damn," Westfall grunted as he lost another hand.

"Gee. Sorry, Mayor," Vivian sighed, leaning toward the blubbery hulk. "The cards fall like the great card player in the sky wants them to."

"Oh, I'm not angry with you, Susanna. It's just that I hate to lose."

"Don't we all," the hotel owner said, showing no sympathy for the defeated mayor.

"Tell you what, Oscar. I'll buy you a drink," Vivian added. "It's about time for a break anyhow."

"Hey," the hotel owner groaned. "I'm hot. You can't leave now."

"Just hang on to your skivvies, Henry." She got up and ruffled the hotel owner's gray hair. "I'll send Melinda over to relieve me."

Henry blushed to a beet-red glow, and the gang around the table was still funning the hotel owner when Vivian and Westfall found an empty table at the back of the room.

"What'll you have, Mayor?" Vivian asked as she reached out and placed her warm hand on his.

"Draught."

"Two beers," Vivian said after getting the bartender's attention.

Vivian easily took the hog-jowled mayor through

two rounds of beer, forced laughter, and moderate touching. Just as things began to drag, he told her the first of several smutty stories. Vivian pretended to respond to the mayor's odd sex chatter with a series of moans and groans accented with bedroom eyes. Halfway through a gusty tale about a girl he knew who could only come when sandwiched between two men, Vivian decided to move before she lost control and fell off her chair in a fit of laughter.

"Excuse me, Oscar. I just realized it's later than I thought. I promised to see Sherm in his office. I was supposed to be there fifteen minutes ago."

"You won't be seeing Sherm for a while," Westfall wheezed. "Now, let me tell you. This girl would take one in either end, and—"

"But I promised," she interrupted, as she set her drink on the dark blue cloth which was draped over the side of the table.

"He's busy. I saw some people come in earlier," Westfall went on as he put a chunky hand on her thigh. "Believe me."

"Oooo. Oscar, you devil," Vivian said as she leaned on his arm with her firm breast. "You this way with all the girls!"

"Most aren't as pretty as you, Susanna," Westfall said, with white pasty saliva forming at the corners of his mouth. "That's the gospel."

"But I told Sherm I'd see him at seven-thirty."

"Take my word for it," Westfall said as he began to stroke her leg. "He'll be tied up."

"Oh. Those two who came in earlier," she said with a knowing look in her eyes. "The dapper tall man and the stumpy-looking dude."

"Yep!"

"The short one looks mean," Vivian said as she put her hand on Westfall's leg. "He must eat nails for breakfast."

"Judd Hall," Westfall volunteered, having no idea that the name had been expertly extracted. "He'd kill you for a fifty-cent piece. If I had my way, the son-of-a-bitch would hang. Killed four I know of."

"You're the mayor!" Vivian exclaimed with a fake tone of shock. "Why don't you have the sheriff arrest him?"

Westfall sighed and didn't answer. His face became a mask of defeat. Vivian decided to increase the tempo of her interrogation by sliding her hand up to the bulge in Westfall's pants. Westfall gasped as she reached the oblong mound and squeezed.

"Seems to me you run the town," she went on.

"A mayor can't do everything he wants," Westfall said, his body momentarily frozen by Vivian's electric touch. "Hall's Traber's muscle and Traber pretty much runs certain things in Tucson."

"Ooo, Oscar. Sounds to me like you know everything that goes on in Tucson," she said as she stroked the stiff rod, which was partly covered by his overhanging gut. "You might be able to help a girl get ahead in this world."

Westfall couldn't talk any longer, as he was

overcome with the artful touch of Susanna Duncan. He began to dig his chubby fingers into her dress and underthings, groping ineptly for the right spot between her legs as he made odd sounds with his short breaths, the foam in the corners of his mouth growing more sticky.

"This Traber's the boss man?" she said, pulling his meat in quick, hard strokes.

"Yeah," he gasped, paralyzed by her hand. "Nothing ahh . . . happens in Tucson that he doesn't ah . . . get in on."

Out of control now, the fat mayor hiked her skirt and found warm flesh. Trying to look somewhat composed, he fumbled his way toward her prize. Torn between disgust and a sense of the absurd, she pumped Westfall fast and firm, after first looking to see if others were staring. In seconds, Westfall shuddered and Vivian felt a warm dampness through his pants.

"Oscar! We can't do this here, for God's sake," she said as his fat finger found her womanhood. "Your friend Henry is looking this way," she lied as she backed away and dropped her hold on his limp and damp cock. "Let's get together some time when we can go to bed," she whispered in his pink ear. "Sometime when we can spend hours with our bodies," she purred, nearly laughing at the idiotic and distant look on his chubby face. "Maybe later in the week."

Westfall began to regain his composure at the

thought that the hotel owner was watching. He figured that it would be just like Henry to make some wisecrack at the next church supper. Most likely, he'd do it right in front of my wife, Westfall thought to himself.

"And besides," Vivian said as she discreetly wiped her hand on the dark-blue tablecloth. "I've got to get back to work. Let's talk later."

Vivian got up and went quickly toward the stairs, once again amused at how easy it was to wrangle a two-hundred-and-eight-pound man by simply holding onto his sausage. She began to smile, until she had a vision of the white spittle in the corners of his mouth. That killed the smile.

Somewhat disgusted with herself, she hammered loudly on Jarrott's door with her knuckles. When the casino owner opened the door, she entered boldly, brushing by Jarrott.

"Susanna! Please! Can't you see I'm busy!"

"Oh. Sorry, Sherm. Didn't know you had company," she said, her expression leaving no doubt as to her honesty. "Just wanted to suggest a late dinner at Eaton's. But I'll see you later." As she turned to leave, she apologized to the two men for her intrusion.

"Sure," Jarrott said. "Later. I'm busy now."

Vivian thought it odd that the usually cool Jarrott seemed upset in the presence of the slender visitor and his muscle man.

"Sherm!" Traber said. "Don't be so quick to send away a beautiful lady."

Vivian thought she saw a veiled message as Traber's eyes passed by those of the pug-nosed bodyguard. Nonetheless, she kept her eyes fixed on Traber.

"You didn't tell me you hired a new girl. Trying to keep her all to yourself?"

"She's one hell of a dealer," Jarrott said. "Fingers faster than a rifle bullet."

Vivian sensed that Traber's good humor was *too* sincere, and she raised her guard. There was something about the smile that shone from under his gray handlebar mustache. His eyes were narrow slits and set far apart by two deep vertical wrinkles just above his sharp nose. Three long wrinkles across his forehead made him look as if he was frowning, a sharp contrast with the square teeth that beamed through thin, smiling lips. She decided that he simply had one of *those* faces.

"Susanna," Jarrott continued. "Like you to meet two business associates. Floyd Traber and Judd Hall."

Traber nodded without altering his strange smile, and Hall touched the brim of his hat.

"Susanna worked the Barbary Coast until an unfortunate political squabble got her boss in trouble," Jarrott explained. "San Francisco's bad luck was my good fortune."

"You must have run into Denny O'Riley, then?" Traber said.

"You must mean Denny O'Brien, Mr. Traber," Vivian said, allowing a smile that signaled Traber that she'd caught on to his amateurish interrogation.

"The Emperor must still be up to his old tricks," Jarrott continued.

Vivian thought fast, her heart skipping a beat. She'd only worked two small scams in San Francisco before the law had caused her and her partner to make an unscheduled departure in the middle of the night. Then it hit her. "Norton the First!" she exclaimed. "Last I knew, he was still printing money."

"Beautiful city," Traber said wistfully. "There was a place—"

"Mr. Traber," Vivian said bluntly. "Do I sense that I am under interrogation?"

"Susanna," Jarrott groaned, obviously distressed by her challenge.

"It's all right, Sherm. Pays to be careful. I don't mind the lady's feisty manner. It's a refreshing change."

Vivian smiled and looked toward Judd Hall. His face remained stone, bent nose and all.

After several minutes of small talk, Traber popped out of his chair and motioned to his hired thug. He daintily kissed Vivian's hand, and the pair departed with no further fanfare.

"Damn, Susanna. I wish you hadn't barged in like that!" Jarrott said the moment they'd gone.

"Sherm," Vivian pouted as she stepped forward and encircled the casino owner with her arms. "I just wanted to see if you were interested in a late dinner."

"No harm done," Jarrott said, becoming his old

self now that the wiry white-haired man had departed. He took off his glasses and set them on his desk.

"Why does he make you so tense?" she asked as she walked behind Jarrott.

"He doesn't bother me!" Jarrott insisted.

Vivian grabbed the firm muscle in his shoulder and began to massage his back.

"You've got a strong back," Vivian said in a sonorous voice. Though her opinion of him had fallen because of his sheepish performance in front of the two visitors, he was still a desirable hunk of man. After soiling her hands earlier, she figured she might as well proceed to soften up Jarrott. Traber and the stumpy bodyguard, she assumed, must know everything Jarrott does. She doubted that the casino owner had the guts to keep *anything* from the slit-eyed crime boss.

After a minute, Jarrott rolled away from her grasp and pulled her into his arms. Then he leaned forward and gently touched his lips to hers. She encouraged him by pressing her pelvis hard against his hardening member and probing his mouth with her tongue. Jarrott's gentleness was soon reduced to animal urgency, and he pulled her dress over her shoulder and down far enough to cause a breast to spring free. His lips left her mouth and clamped on an erect nipple.

"Oooo. God, Sherm, that feels good," Vivian groaned as she toyed with the long, curly and soft hair on the back of his head. "But Sherm . . . Oooo," she went on, only partly acting. "But we can't do anything tonight. I'm . . . sorry."

"What?" Jarrott said, dropping the nipple from his lips.

"Bad time of the month. And I'm cursed with a horrible flow."

"Jesus," Jarrott moaned.

She figured that he would be squeamish, and for that she was thankful. She wanted to work him up to it slowly. She wanted to hold off long enough to fog up his mind with desire so that he might become slack and say something he shouldn't.

"Sorry," she said, backing away and gently and slowly palming her breast back into her dress.

Jarrott was bug-eyed at the sight of the slender hand tucking away the large firm orb.

Vivian smiled. *Magic,* she thought to herself. Then something made her think of Judd Hall and his devil eyes. She guessed that he was one man who wouldn't be fooled by *magic*.

NINE

Ain't been here an hour and I'm sweatin' like a whore in church," Kirk muttered from his position on a small ledge.

"Shut up, Kirk!" Pearl shouted. "That goddamned stage will be here any minute. And keep that square head of yours *down!*"

Tallman wiped the sweat from his brow and replaced his hat. He smiled at the way Pearl commanded her troops. She'd give any experienced Army major a run for his money. "Some woman," he muttered to himself as he looked down on the narrow and steep upgrade. There was no better place for an ambush in all of Picacho Pass. He wondered what she might have done if she had set her mind and energy to earning an honest living. As it was, he was out to see her hang. And there was no profit in that.

"Here they come," Pearl said, just as Tallman heard the faint thunder of twenty-four hooves. "Do like you have been told, and no one will get hurt!"

Tallman's heart began to speed up as the noise of the stage grew louder. He was acutely aware that he was in the midst of a bunch of half-crazed killers. And he remembered Pearl's warning about the Wells Fargo guard. Anything could happen.

Just as the team of six snorting and straining horses rounded the final bend at a slow trot, Doc jumped into the middle of the road and leveled his Winchester on the guard. Tallman, positioned on a high vantage point, behind a row of boulders, had been told to take a bead on the guard and kill him if it even looked like he was going for Doc.

"Stop!" Doc shouted to the driver, his voice serious and tense. "One move and you'll be eatin' lunch with the devil."

The driver instinctively reined in the horses when he caught sight of the man in the road.

Then Tallman saw the guard thumb the double hammers on his shotgun. Hoping to avoid killing, he fired at the top of the guard's hat. Thanks to his skill and a dash of luck, the guard's hat flew as if snatched by a fly fisherman's errant cast. "Don't move mister," Tallman growled as the shotgunner looked in the direction of the blast. "I'll put the next one in your goddamn ear!"

The wide-eyed guard set the double barrel in his lap and slowly moved his hands away from the weapon.

"Clear," Tallman shouted.

Then Jake and Pearl stepped from the large fissure that had been their cover. Like the rest of the gang, she had a bandanna on her face. But her large hat was pulled down over her eyes, she'd bound her chest in torn bedsheets, and she said nothing. Jake held the horses and trained his revolver on the driver, while Pearl held her Remington on the guard.

"Clear," Doc shouted to Kirk.

Once he'd heard Doc's voice, Kirk hopped down off a waist-high ledge behind the stage and ran forward with the two-foot crowbar. As he approached the coach, Doc moved to the door and ordered the two passengers to get out and lie face down in the road. The older of the two had a dark, weathered face and was dressed like a lifelong miner. He seemed unmoved by the unfolding robbery. The other, obviously some sort of itinerant peddler, was scared white and breathless.

As the salesman went face down, Pearl calmly walked around the far side of the coach. Without warning, she quickly raised her .36-caliber Remington and shot the Wells Fargo guard in the side. The team jumped, each horse straining to go its own way, and the guard pitched forward and fell seven feet to the road.

Tallman froze, his mind momentarily dulled by the savage act.

"Goddamn," Kirk grunted in a matter-of-fact

tone when he saw the guard hit the dirt. As the man began writhing, churning up a small pool of red mud, Kirk looked in Pearl's glazed eyes, once again amazed at how she could pleasure at such a sight. Then she leveled the .36 on the man's crotch and fired again, sending a slug into his balls. Kirk, having had enough of her savagery, jumped into the coach and began prying up the coach floor.

When Tallman heard the second shot, the ghastly grunting that followed, and then saw the guard's boot heel digging at the road, he had to make a snap decision. Though he couldn't see where Pearl had shot the man, it was obvious that her lead was meant to torture, not to kill. He was in a position to revenge the brutal act and stop the gang for good. From his perch, he could kill Jake, Kirk, and Doc in an instant and hope for a better shot at Pearl. But he was sure that the people at the top would find more highwaymen with little effort.

"Hurry up!" Jake shouted as the restless team tugged at his grip. "Goddamn horses are gettin' skittish."

Cursing the decision, Tallman decided to accept the grisly scene. However, at that moment, he swore he'd not rest until Pearl and her boys were fitted for a pine suit or awaiting the hangman's trapdoor.

In only a few minutes, Kirk had ripped up the floorboards and thrown the heavy box out of the right side of the coach.

"Hey, boys!" Doc bellowed from the other side of the stage. "The drummer just pissed his britches. Think I ought to shoot the son-of-a-bitch!"

No one answered Stroud, as Jake was busy with the six horses and Pearl and Kirk were intent on opening the strongbox. Pearl fired three slugs into the locked brass latch before it fell from the hardwood box. Kirk bent over and lifted the lid.

"Well, ain't that pretty," Kirk said as he spied eight canvas bags bulging with coin.

Pearl snatched four of the bags and headed for the cleft in the rocks. Kirk sensed her urgency and followed suit, stepping wide of the guard, whose eyes burned with pain and helplessness as his bootheel continued to dig.

After Kirk and Pearl had vanished, Doc eyeballed the driver. "See that feller up in them rocks?" he said as he pointed to Tallman. "He's going to keep you in his sights for a few minutes. You seen how he shot the man's hat off, so you know he can shoot you in the fucking ear if he wants," Doc went on, enjoying his speech. "And you, drummer! Stop your goddamned cryin' before I shoot you in the asshole for givin' manhood a bad name. Keep quiet like your buddy here." Then he kicked the blubbering traveler in the side, signaled Jake to back away, and moved toward the slit in the rocks.

Tallman wondered if the scarfaced Doc Stroud would give manhood a bad name when they walked him up the stairs to see the hangman. "Probably piss a river," he said quietly. In his day, he'd seen a few Doc Strouds approach the gallows, and most did.

As Jake, Doc, and Kirk slugged popskull rye and laughed about the drummer who'd peed his pants, Tallman sat quietly, sipping his cheap whiskey, and watching Pearl carefully arrange the stacks of coins into three distinct groups. She fondled the metal as a mother might touch a newborn child.

"Gaawd damn," she finally said, her words sounding oddly like an orgiastic moan. "Twenty-four thousand! Just like the man said. That makes eight for you boys." Her words were soft and her eyes were locked on the yellow metal.

"How does that tickle your fancy, Hoodoo?" Doc whooped after Pearl had divided the money. "Not bad for a day's work."

"Damn sure ain't," Tallman agreed, his mind still distracted by Pearl's earlier display of cruelty.

"Well, boys! What do you say? Think Red Rock's ready for us?" Doc literally shouted after he tossed back another shot of popskull. "You ready to celebrate, Hoodoo?"

"Hoodoo's stayin' here tonight," Pearl announced with a smile. "Me and him's goin' to get to know each other a little better."

"Wheeeew," Doc jested. "I'd say a whole lot better."

"Goddamn," Kirk moaned in a kidding tone. "Poor Hoodoo's never gonna forget tonight."

"Shut up, you fuck-ups," Pearl groaned as she kicked Kirk in the ass. "All three of you pecker-woods! Get the hell out of here!"

Tallman watched the unusual display of human action with some amusement. The trio hooted and hollered, taunting Pearl like three little kids toying with their mother. Three kiddies and their sadistic mama.

"And I don't want to see none of you until tomorrow," she shouted from the cabin step as they walked toward the lopsided barn.

"Looks like those boys will tear Red Rock to the ground this evening," Tallman said from his chair as he eyeballed the lady killer. "Just about drunk already."

Pearl closed the door, took two steps, stopped, and gave Tallman an odd stare. After a pause, she spoke. "How come you didn't gun that guard?" she asked bluntly, her hand resting on her .36 Remington. "This ain't no trick-shootin' carnival act, Hoodoo!"

"Goddamn, lady!" Tallman shot back. "There wasn't no need for it. No reason to make that man suffer like that and no reason to piss Wells Fargo off any more than necessary."

"I don't want no arguments," she said as she threw aside her hat, and began to undo her hair. "I want them stagecoach shotgunners scared to death. Next time, shoot the bastard in the head . . . like you done the kid."

Tallman built a smoke and offered no arguments.

From her bent perspective, her reasoning was sound. The gunshot guard would be plenty of warning if he made it back to Tucson alive. It was his job to shut down the whole operation as soon as possible, and that meant more play-acting with the little scorpion, Pearl Bowen.

"Otherwise, Hoodoo, you done good," she said as she approached him and began to unbutton her calico shirt. "Figure you can handle a real woman like you do that six-shooter of yours?"

Tallman gave her a knowing grin and took a deep pull on his cigarette.

The little woman undid the last button on her shirt and stripped it away, revealing a chest wrapped with several strips of torn bedsheet. "How about you unwrap me before my tits are squashed permanent," she said as she eyed the newcomer.

"Be glad to, Pearl." Tallman allowed an inward smile as he walked over and untied the knots. The little woman aroused him, and he thought that odd when he considered her potential for brutality and her deranged view of the world. At once, he wondered if there was some strange animalistic mutual attraction between them. But he quickly wrote off that theory and accepted the fact that almost any woman can arouse a man if she was willing to work at it. He recalled one homely woman who was ten years his senior and a hundred pounds overweight, a Quaker who worked the underground during the Civil War. Few women, before or since, had aroused his sex as expertly as she had. When he undid the last wrap, Pearl began to rub her breasts with a slow circular motion.

"What do you think, Hoodoo?" she asked as she turned to face him. "Nice tits for a woman two years shy of forty. Wouldn't you say?"

Tallman looked at the small, firm orbs, which were topped by the longest nipples he'd ever seen. He nodded approval.

Pearl put a finger through his bandanna, turned, and pulled him toward the bedroom. His first instinct was to break her finger off and stuff it up her ass, but he held his temper and played along.

"Stand still," she said when they got in the room. Her voice sounded feminine for the first time since he'd met her.

"What is it you got in mind, Pearl?" Tallman asked.

"Sex," she purred. "My way."

"You're the boss," he said as he reached for the small breasts. "Nice."

Pearl stood back, popped her feet out of her boots, and slowly squirmed out of the loose-fitting jeans. Tallman's interest soared when he saw shapely legs topped with a jutting ass and a curly triangle of hair, which did nothing to cover the bulging lips that clearly delineated her womanhood.

"Shame you hide that under them duds all the time," he said, his cock growing hard.

Pearl came closer and stroked the lump in his

pants. "Totin' a spare barrel for your Colt, Hoodoo?"

While she deftly undid his belt and buttons, he fingered her unusual nipples. He took one of the little knobs, twirled it, and pulled gently. Pearl dropped his pants, snatched his purple-veined cock from his drawers and stared lovingly at the one-eyed monster as she stroked it.

"Get the rest of your clothes off," she whispered as she dropped his throbbing meat and backed out of his hold on her breasts.

While Tallman kicked his boots off and stepped out of his pants, Pearl went to her bed, fell supine, and spread her legs as far as they would go. With her eyes fixed on Tallman, she smiled and, with both hands, pulled the lips of her cunt as far apart as they'd go. "You like this?" she asked. "Nice pink meat?"

"Never seen one I didn't," Tallman answered, feeling somewhat foolish.

Then she broadened her smile, released one side, stuck her finger deep into her own moist bog and began to moan, all the while keeping her eyes fixed on his.

Tallman, his rod engorged with blood, went to the bed and prepared to mount her. She stopped him.

"My way. Remember? Now lay down," she said quietly as she turned to her side.

Tallman obliged the lady robber and fell on his back, his swollen member pointing skyward. Pearl got up, sat next to him Indian style, grabbed his stiff cock firmly and began pumping with one hand as she palmed his balls with the other.

Tallman watched as she stroked rhythmically and stared at her work. "I love to watch a man shoot," she said in a monotone. "Just be still and let me do everything."

Not having had a woman in days, Tallman was quickly aroused, and her careful attention to her task was bringing him rapidly toward his release. She sensed his growing desire and placed her middle finger on his anus and poked at his sphincter until she pushed beyond the tight valve and began to massage his prostate with her fingertip.

Tallman was being taken with the sensation and he began to move against her hand and finger. Pearl, sensing Tallman's arousal, tightened her grip, stroked faster, and probed deeper. Tallman grunted as her deft fingers unleashed his seed. The head of his cock erupted in a shower of lumpy, white juice. A second convulsion sent another load aloft. Then a third. Tallman couldn't believe the sensation. It was unlike anything he'd ever experienced, though he did feel sheepish as he came down from the orgiastic high, and became acutely aware of her nimble finger in his ass. He moved his eyes from the timber rafters to her face. Her eyes were glazed as she continued to pump out the final drops. She had the distant look of a lunatic.

Her odd stare made him go limp.

Sensing that his cock was softening, she bent

forward, removed her finger from his hole, and captured the dying organ in her thin-lipped mouth, sucking and working his tip with her hard tongue. No man would have wilted under the skillful mouth of Pearl Bowen. Her tongue lashed at the hardening shaft, her head bobbed rhythmically, and the room came alive with the sound of greedy sucking. As she stroked him with her tight lips, she moaned loudly and flung her leg over his supine body and sat on his chest, her buttocks toward his face. Then she dropped him from her mouth, scooted forward, grabbed his ankles, raised herself and straddled his erect manhood. Very slowly, with perfect aim, she lowered herself on his shaft.

Tallman craned his neck foward and watched as his huge cock disappeared into her damp curls. Once it had vanished, she slowly raised herself until the tip was about to pop out. Then she went slowly down again. As she pumped the tempo increased, and soon, she was hammering him with the speed of a piston on a fast-moving locomotive. Just as they were both rising toward trembling release, the sounds of a rider pierced the walls of the cabin.

"Jesus Christ," Pearl moaned, as she quickly removed herself from his pole. "That son-of-a-bitch would have to show right now."

TEN

Tallman caught up with Doc the next evening just after sundown. The scarfaced outlaw was running amok in Anita's, Red Rock's only sporting house.

"Figured you'd be somewhere where you could grease your pole," Tallman said as he spotted the half-bagged stage robber, who had a fifteen-year-old Mexican whore sitting on his lap.

"Hoodoo!" Doc shouted across the parlor when he saw Tallman.

Tallman made his way through the liquored-up patrons and their scantily clothed attendants. At Stroud's table, he pulled out a chair and sat down.

"Have a drink, Hoodoo," Stroud said, his lips thick with whiskey. "And some of this," he added as he reached into the girl's loose dress and pulled out a youthful breast. As Stroud drunkenly pawed the girl's tit and plucked the dark brown nipple, the young whore, who had the eyes of a moron, giggled like a ten-year-old.

"You kiddin', Doc!" Tallman grunted as he poured a shot of sourmash. "Pearl wore me out proper last night. Goddamn woman's crazy."

"Crazy don't describe Pearl," Doc laughed as he greedily pawed at the little firm breast. "There ain't no words to say how she is."

"You ain't shittin'!" Tallman added as he took out the makings of a smoke. "Once with that bitch is all I want. Got me enough of a stake to lay back a bit. Play some cards."

"You ain't ridin' with us again?"

"Nope," Tallman said as he stroked a sulphurhead on the underside of the scratched table. "You and Kirk and Jake can have her all to yourselves." Tallman was anxious to move on to Tucson without causing any suspicion or ill feelings among the outlaws.

"Jesus," Doc moaned. He dropped the girl's breast and rubbed his scarred cheek. He suddenly appeared to sober. "I don't know if Pearl's gonna like that."

"She ain't got no choice in the matter," Tallman said firmly as he eyed Doc with a serious expression. "Woman's trouble. You boys mark my words." Tallman laughed inwardly. "I don't mind stealin' from them bastards at Wells Fargo. But I ain't gonna be party to the likes of what she done to that guard."

Doc just looked at Tallman with lazy eyes.

The whore jiggled her tit with her tiny hand. "You boys like?" she asked dumbly. "One dollar."

Tallman made small talk with Doc and the idiot whore while he downed a final shot of whiskey. When an Oriental in see-through silk approached, he begged off, claiming that he was planning to spend all night at a poker table in Tucson. The sore on the upper lip of the Chinese girl confirmed his first impression—Anita's was the kind of place where one could get a permanent case of bugs on the brain.

"Pearl ain't gonna like it," Doc said as Tallman got up. "I'm tellin' you, she might take it personal-like."

"You no stay fuck Ling Chan?" the Oriental asked Tallman.

Tallman tipped his hat at the *putas* and walked off. As he threaded his way through the dimly lit parlor and out the door, he pondered the half-dressed flesh sprawled on the cheap furniture. The scene caused him to reflect on his evening with Pearl. After she'd interrupted her backwards mount at the sound of the rider, she dressed, met the rider outside, and passed on what appeared to be a third of the gold. While she jawed briefly with the rider, he had quietly made his way to the front window. Being careful to avoid detection, he'd gotten a look at the rider and his distinctive brown-on-white paint. But from his vantage point beside the window, he'd been unable to hear anything but mumbling. When she'd returned to the bedroom . . . Well, he thought to himself as he mounted his horse and recalled Pearl's odd sexual behavior, at least she didn't send *me* for the bacon grease.

As he headed south under the cool, early evening air, he slowly began to further ponder a plan that would rid the countryside of Pearl's gang and those higher up in the organization.

It was just past ten when he entered Tucson. It had been a year since he'd seen the territorial capital, and he was taken with its sprawling growth. He turned his horse over to the Mexican in the livery at the end of Calle de San Miguel and headed back to the Buena Suerte after he'd inquired as to the whereabouts of Sherm Jarrott. As he made the five-block trip, he found amusement in the throngs of men who were out that evening to win a fortune, or to vent their manhood in the belly of a whore, or to get stone-head drunk . . . or all three. When he saw the gaming joint on the other side of the street, he made his way across the dusty hardpan, hoping that Vivian had made some headway. Truth be known, he still needed more—much more—to solve Wells Fargo's problem.

When he entered the smoke-filled gambling den, he at once caught sight of Vivian's table. She was tending to four boisterous players, and her table was surrounded by a host of rubberneckers who were hooting and laughing at the expense of a red-faced fat man. He smiled at the scene, walked to the bar, bellied up to the polished wood, and ordered a beer.

He nursed the cold suds as he made his way to the casino's most popular table. Shortly after he had arrived, a drunken sodbuster lost his last silver dollar and left the game, wondering what he'd tell his wife about the disposition of the month's allowance for provisions. Tallman snatched the empty chair and began to lose. With a perfectly straight face she took his money on every bet. Some sense of humor, he mused. Despite her expensive amusement, she managed to get a cryptic message to her fellow Pinkerton. She'd see him later that evening in the Governor Hotel. Then he began to win. Sixty dollars to the good. Tallman left the game, hoping to get some shuteye before the 4 A.M. closing.

His mind adrift, he ambled through the stained-glass doors and went left on the plankwalk. After only two blocks, he was alerted by a passing horse. It was the paint he'd seen from the window the night before. He kept walking and followed the loping horseman. In less than a minute, the rider tied his mount to a hitching rail in front of Vincent's Saloon. The man who'd taken delivery of the gold stopped before entering and surveyed the street.

Oddly, he and Tallman locked eyes for an instant even though they were separated by the width of the busy street. Though it was only a momentary thing, Tallman cursed himself, somehow concerned that the man was sharp enough to make something of it.

But the rider seemed undaunted as he spun on his heels and entered Vincent's. Tallman waited for five minutes and crossed the street. At the edge of the front window of the saloon, he checked for the rider. The nameless man appeared to be nowhere in the bar. He waited ten minutes to assure himself that the man was not in the outhouse, and then he went into the bar. There were no women, and the bartender denied that he had any cribs. Concerned, Tallman went outside with the idea of establishing a watch over the man's horse. The handsome mount had vanished.

For the next four hours, Tallman walked the streets in search of the distinctive paint. His efforts were fruitless. Discouraged by the sour luck, he went back to the Buena Suerte and waited for Vivian. When she emerged from the casino, he followed her to her hotel. With the exception of a few stumbling drunks, the moonlit street was quiet.

"Who is it?" Vivian asked after hearing the light knocking sound at her door.

"Ash."

"Come on in," she said quietly after she opened the door.

"You look good, Viv," Tallman said as he threw his hat on the bed. "A sight for sore eyes."

"What did you find out?" Vivian asked eagerly. She was obviously engrossed in the case.

"Enough. But we need more to nail the coffin shut on the higher-ups. Even pulled a job the day before yesterday. I damn near closed the case right then and there." He paused and gave her a serious look. "Watch your step. We're dealing with a bad bunch."

"I know," she sighed. "It's all over town about that Wells Fargo guard! Who the hell shot his balls off?"

"The leader of the bunch. A snake named Pearl Bowen."

"A woman?"

"Meaner than a cornered wildcat."

"You can't get much meaner than what she did. They say the man has better than a fifty-fifty chance. At least that's what I heard."

Tallman winced, thinking of the cold-blooded way Pearl gutshot the guard and then blasted his crotch.

"Like I said," Tallman went on with raised eyebrows. *"Be careful!"*

"That bitch ought to be drawn and quartered," Vivian said through clenched teeth.

"That would be too good for her," Tallman said. "Even the Indians couldn't make her pay her dues. But for now let's forget Pearl Bowen and her gang of mama's boys. What have you been able to get?"

"I found out who Jarrott reports to. A man named Floyd Traber. I have nothing to tie him to the Wells Fargo jobs, but he is the number-one crook in Tucson. So I doubt he misses much. Travels with a dog-faced bodyguard who's built like a tree stump. Also, Jarrott has me stroking the mayor of Tucson. I'm on orders to keep him up by sixty or seventy dollars a week. Might be a slick sort of payoff. But, to be honest, I don't think the mayor has the sense to know whether or not he's winning or losing."

Tallman listened and began to roll a cigarette. "Be glad when I can go back to factory-made smokes," he said. "So you got anything more on Traber?"

"Nothing more than I've just told you. I figure that my next step is to get next to Traber. He was bug-eyed the other night when I showed him a little of this," she said as she squeezed her arms and caused a blossom of cleavage. "So it won't be long."

"A man would have to be queer to resist."

Vivian ducked her chin and raised her eyebrows as she walked to the bed. Though she was able to ignore all convention and use the mysteries of the flesh to dangle most men at the end of a string, Tallman stirred her juices in a different way. She was drawn to his animal magnetism, his self-assurance, and the calm determination with which he marched to his own drummer. She felt her face flush as she sat on the bed, took the half-burned cigarette from his hand and squashed it in the hammered-brass ashtray. She pulled him back on the goose down and gently pressed her warm soft lips to his, her tongue gently probing. She backed off to say something, when he clamped his hand over her mouth.

"Quiet!" he whispered, his voice overflowing with urgency. "I heard something at the door."

As he rolled quietly off the bed, he snatched his

Colt from its leather. Once his feet were firmly on the floor, he bolted from the bed and opened the door. He caught a glimpse of a man disappearing down the staircase, three steps at a time. He knew the snoop.

"We got trouble," he said in a rapid-fire voice.

"What!"

"Someone at the door," he said as he grabbed his hat and holster. "I'll talk to you tomorrow."

Tallman darted into the street, which was illuminated by the light-gray pre-dawn eastern sky. He saw nothing, but on instinct he turned right and began to move slowly toward Tucson's vice district. If he didn't find the man who rode the distinctive brown-on-white paint, he'd have to close the case, putting only Pearl and her bunch out of action. Just as he was passing the first alley, a drunk stirred on the plankwalk on the other side of the street. Tallman turned, leveling his drawn revolver in the direction of the sound.

"One move, mister," a voice said from the shadows in the alley at his back. "Even breathe heavy and you'll die screamin'."

"Easy does it," Tallman said. "I ain't got no money."

"Not your money I'm interested in. Now back into this here alley and don't try to move that hogleg."

Tallman did what he was told.

"Now drop that Colt," the man ordered, once

Tallman had backed into the shadows. "Easy like."

Tallman winced as the fine weapon thunked in the dirt.

"Now how about you turn around and tell me what you are doin' in Tucson. First I seen you followin' me earlier, and now I hear you talkin' bullshit about Jarrott and Traber with that lady card slick."

"Got somethin' against a man gettin' a piece of ass?" Tallman growled at the nameless rider, hoping for some sort of edge.

"Seems to me like you got more than a piece of ass goin' with the dealer. Sounded like detective talk to me. What say we go over and see Mr. Traber so's you can explain about your piece of ass to him. Somethin' tells me that when I tell him what I heard, you ain't goin' to see no more sunsets." The rider sounded as if he could and would kill at the slightest provocation. "Now move!"

Tallman, surmising that the rider had talked to no one, decided he had to make a move now or die later. As he turned to walk away, he pressed his forearm to his side. The hideout rig released the little .41 derringer. He spun away just as the metal hit his palm, leveled the gun, and fired. The little derringer exploded right in the man's chest, the muzzle only inches away. The shot made only an eerie thump, silenced by clothing and exploding meat. Tallman's assailant opened his mouth as if to scream, gunsmoke curled from his lips, and he pitched backward as if his legs had been chopped away at the knees. The smoking corpse hit the ground like a grain sack dropped from a six-foot loading platform.

The Pinkerton agent looked carefully around the edge of the building. Satisfied that he'd not been seen, he grabbed his Colt from the dirt and turned to the body.

After several moments of contemplation, he crouched down, turned the outlaw's pockets, and fled with the dead man's coin, billfold, and watch.

ELEVEN

By the time he made his way carefully to the livery, the eastern sky was light, outlining the eight-thousand-foot peaks of the Rincón Range. At the well behind the stable, he raised a bucket of water and washed several spots of gelled blood from his hand and face. After cleaning up, he dropped the dead man's watch in the well and buried the billfold deep in the steamy manure pile after pocketing the banknotes and coin.

Assured that he had erased any trace of his part in the killing, he entered the barn, walked quietly past the snoring Mexican, looked in on his horse, and then retrieved his bedroll and saddlebags from the warped wooden shelf next to the rack that held his saddle.

After a twenty-minute walk, he found a suitable four-bit hotel and strolled casually into the lobby.

"You come with the sun, *señor,*" the desk clerk said cheerfully.

"Something like that, *amigo,*" Tallman muttered. "How about a room?"

"*Sí, señor*. Feefty cents. One night."

"Got a bath?"

The clerk pointed to a door across from the desk. "Feefty cents."

"Make the bath hot and use fresh water and you can keep the change," Tallman said as he thumped two silver dollars on the marred wooden counter.

"Síii, señor," the clerk responded as he put one dollar in the tin box under the counter and the other in his pocket. *"Quince minutos."*

After a bath, a shave, and a long breakfast, Tallman made his way to Commercial Street and bought a dark-gray pinstripe suit, a black bowler, lace-up high-top shoes, several shirts, and a fancy suit bag made of supple brown leather.

Back in his hotel room, he carefully slicked back his hair after adding a wisp of gray to either side. Using spirit gum, he then attached a stubby gray-red mustache. His plain-glass silver-wire spectacles in place, he stood back from the mirror and chuckled out loud at his handiwork. Over the years he had become a master of disguise and an actor worthy of any big-city stage production. Aside from the risk, the money, and the fast-changing pace of life his work provided, he found great amusement in casting himself as a hard case, an inept drummer, or some vain, blowhard captain of industry and finance. *Doing good* was, of course, not a moving force in his life. His mission was a far cry from a personal crusade to rid the world of the likes of Pearl Bowen and her little kiddies. He jammed an expensive cigar in the corner of his mouth and laughed once more at what he saw in the mirror.

Once he had attached the .41 hideout derringer and had stuffed his stubby .41 Colt New Line into its spring-loaded leather, he donned the dark-gray jacket and straightened the black-and-maroon bow tie. The black bowler completed the transformation. He *was* Cyrus Purdy, Chicago mining speculator.

His disguise complete, he stuffed his long-barrel revolver, holster, boots, and other things into the new suit bag and quietly departed the third-rate hotel by the back stairs.

An hour later Cyrus Purdy had registered at the Governor Hotel and settled into his room.

"Mr. Oldham in?" Tallman asked the clerk at the shipping desk. It was fifteen minutes after noon.

"Yes . . . but . . ."

"Well, I'll just surprise him," Tallman said as he walked toward Oldham's office door with the well-practiced strut of someone important. "Can't be too busy to see an old friend."

Tallman opened the door and entered the office before the elderly clerk had backed away from his paper-cluttered desk.

"It's me. Tallman," he whispered as he closed the door.

Oldham, momentarily taken aback, quickly regained his composure when he understood.

"Cyrus Purdy, mining speculator."

"I daresay you look like one," Oldham chuckled. "That's a hell of a getup."

After they exchanged greetings and a minute of small talk, Tallman launched into an explanation of what had unfolded since their meeting in Santa Fe.

"Traber," Oldham repeated quietly as he nodded up and down. "You might have something there. Though I can't think of any connection between Traber and anyone in my office."

"What do you know about the man?"

"Nothing for sure. But the rumors run hot and fast. Most say he's Tucson's vice czar. Takes a cut on all the saloons, whorehouses, and gaming dives. Word has it that he is in deep with the politicos down at the courthouse."

Tallman recalled what Vivian had said about the mayor's blackjack winnings as he fired up an expensive cheroot.

"Does the mayor run the town with an iron fist?"

"Not really. He's mostly a backslapper and baby-kisser. Real gasbag. God knows how he gets elected, but he does. I always thought the Trabers and Jarrotts of the world somehow kept him in office. Folks say Oscar Westfall is kept in line with wine, women, and coin. Gather he can't keep his hands off the ladies."

"Can't figure it. Slicks like Traber don't usually

get themselves in that deep," Tallman said as he savored the taste of the slender cigar. "Somehow it's out of character."

"Greed is never out of character, Mr. Tallman."

"You got a point, Perry. Nothing carved in stone that says a whoremaster can't be a stage robber."

Oldham shrugged.

"I'll put money on Traber," Tallman said. "Nothing else to go on at the moment. I'll see you again as soon as I have something to go on."

"You know where to find me." Oldham paused and his face went sour. "One more thing." He looked Tallman in the eyes. "That guard they shot up."

"What about him?"

"He was one of my best men and a good friend. We rode shotgun together years ago. As far as I am concerned, you can plant every one of those bastards and save the cost of a trial."

Tallman tipped his bowler, allowed a wry smile, and left the office.

Sherm Jarrott was leaning on the bar complaining to the barkeep about the recent property-tax increases. He had just finished a cold draught when Traber and his goon walked through the door. The casino owner told the bartender what to deliver and then he led the odd couple to his personal table in the far corner.

Vivian saw Traber's entrance and noted that

Cyrus Purdy entered two minutes later, ordered a beer, and sat in on a poker game not far from Jarrott's table. She smiled at the disguise and felt a surge of warmth in her loins as she recalled the meeting they'd had earlier.

Tallman listened carefully but he could only make out a few words. TRABER: *I don't like it.* JARROTT: . . . *probably . . . took . . . money and watch.* TRABER: . . . *something not right.* HALL: *Murphy never . . . on him.* He assumed that they were talking about the dead messenger. The morning paper had it as a late-night robbery and murder. They'd named the victim as Jimmy Murphy, address unknown. Tallman noticed that Traber had an aura of danger about his skinny frame. He guessed that Traber was as deadly as a coiled diamondback.

Vivian had waited for a half hour before signaling the floor manager for relief.

"Sherm," Vivian said as she approached the private table. "I'm going to take a few minutes to go to my hotel room." Then she turned to Traber. "How are you this evening?"

"Just fine, Susanna. Won't you have a drink with us first? Sherm's got the good stuff out."

"No, thanks, Mr. Traber."

"Floyd," Traber said softly. "Mr. Traber was my father."

Poor son-of-a-bitch, Vivian thought to herself. Imagine a son like *that!* "Maybe later."

"I've got a better idea yet. How about supper at my place?"

"Floyd," Jarrott intervened. "You planning to eat at four A.M.? 'Cause I can't let you have my top dealer till then."

Vivian saw Traber glare at Jarrott for an instant before speaking. "How about eleven?" he asked. "My place."

"I'd love to. But I'll be working late, like Sherm said." She was delighted to be able to drive a wedge between the two.

"Sherm doesn't mind," he said as his eyes shifted from hers to Jarrott's. The bent-nosed tree stump added his malicious stare. "Do you, Sherm?"

"Enjoy yourself," Jarrott said, smiling as he remembered that she had her period. Hope you choke to death on the blood, you skinny fuck, Jarrott thought to himself. He longed for the day when he would build the nerve to kill Traber.

"Well, thank you, Sherm," Vivian said. "Eleven it is, Floyd."

As Vivian walked away from the table, she caught a sly smile in the corner of Tallman's mouth. She could see that he was pleased with her easy moves. She frowned, letting him know that she was not going to find any pleasure in being with the tall, gray-topped snake. The fact that the sharp-nosed vice boss might want to get under her petticoat made her shudder.

TWELVE

Tallman tipped his black bowler at the hotel clerk as he walked past the front desk.

"Morning, Mr. Purdy," the often-tipped clerk answered when he caught the gesture.

The sun was just coming over the mountains as he stepped off the boardwalk to cross the street. The blue sky was void of clouds. He took a deep breath of the morning air and set off to the livery at a brisk walk.

After a ten-minute ride in the rented buggy, he found what he was looking for. A two-foot-long sign, gold leaf on dark blue, hung over the door: TRABER & COMPANY, LTD., REAL ESTATE. The white board-and-batten building was carefully trimmed in the same dark blue that was used on the sign. Numerous potted flowers hung from the porch roof.

Tallman quickly surveyed the street, which was bordered with commercial establishments. He sighed relief when he saw the Poste y Dehesa within sight of the real-estate office. With his stomach begging for a heavy breakfast, he quickly secured the much-used horse and carriage. His run of luck continuing, Tallman got a window seat, found a once-used copy of the morning *Tucson Freeman* on the table, and noticed that the breakfast special was a three-egg cheese-and-chili omelette served with biscuits and a half-pound chunk of tenderloin. Somehow, he never managed a sound meal when on the job. The breakfast would partly make up for that flaw in his line of work.

As he awaited his meal, sipped black coffee, and watched Traber's office, he reflected on his late-night meeting with Vivian. She'd found Traber the perfect gentleman, but she'd learned nothing. They had gone to Tucson's best steak house and talked for two hours about everything but business. Vivian had claimed that her subtle attempts to beguile Traber into loosening his lips had all failed. Sensing something menacing about the wiry vice boss, she had been careful to pry gently.

Just as Tallman was shaking his head in admiration of the way Vivian had taken to the detective business on this, their second assignment, Traber and Judd Hall pulled up to the real-estate office in a buckboard towed by a matched pair of sixteen-hand chestnuts, each with four white stockings. The uncommon duo mounted the steps and disappeared into the building.

Tallman watched the office and savored the tenderloin, the spicy eggs, and the biscuits, hoping Traber would take his time, leaving him enough time to finish the only good meal he'd had in days.

His luck held. Two hours later, the sharp-faced vice czar and his henchman left the real-estate office in the expensive buggy.

Tallman slapped a silver dollar and a quarter on the table in payment of the ninety-cent meal and moved quickly toward the door.

Careful to stay as far from Hall and Traber as possible, he followed them through the now teeming business district to the southwest side of Tucson. After he observed several stops from side streets, it soon became obvious that the pair was making collections. Hall went in alone if the whorehouse or saloon was extremely sleazy, but usually, as a pair, they entered with an air of confidence and determination and came out minutes later counting coin or banknotes. After Traber made a quick entry in a small black book he kept in his vest pocket, they were off to another saloon or gaming dive.

By the time Hall emerged from a place labeled simply DANCE DRINKS, Tallman had had enough. The Arizona sun was beginning to cook his brain.

After they had pulled away, he wheeled his rickety rental buggy and old horse out of the side street from which he had been observing the pair of extortionists and headed back to the restaurant that overlooked Traber's real-estate office. He assumed they would return to Traber's place of business soon, as they had only two or three more stops before they'd covered all the joints in the vice district.

As he was nursing a cold beer and savoring a hot steak, onion, and cheese sandwich, Traber and his flunky tied up the matched pair at the rail in front of the real-estate office. Tallman was sure that Traber was Tucson's vice lord, but he still had nothing to tie the lanky gray-topped man to Pearl Bowen. And time was running short. He recalled Pearl's suggestion that they might have another holdup before the week's end. The food suddenly seemed less appealing as he reflected on the way the guard had tumbled head first from the coach and how she had shot his balls off with not one second of remorse. He mused that she'd look good at the end of a rope . . . if it got that far. As he sipped his beer he wondered if he hadn't got into a box canyon. Without some sort of hard evidence linking Traber, Jarrott, and Pearl, none of the outlaws would ever see the insides of a courthouse. "There are other ways," he said to the table.

"What?" the pretty black-haired waitress asked.

"Nothing," Tallman replied, looking up at the young woman. "Talking to spirits."

"Oh." The girl seemed to believe him. She paused before passing the handsome mining speculator on her way to get him another beer.

Just as he was about to chomp down on the last

bite of the sandwich, Mayor Westfall waddled up the street and into Traber's office.

One and a half beers later, the chubby mayor stepped onto the boardwalk and stuffed a bulky envelope into his vest pocket.

Tallman left money on the red tablecloth and quickly left the Poste y Dehesa. Since Westfall was on foot and the streets were jammed with people, stalking the man was a simple task. Tallman followed the cherub-faced politician to his first stop, the Tucson Safe Deposit & Trust, the town's biggest bank. After a short stop there and numerous sidewalk interruptions for superficial conversations, handshakes, and backslapping, he made his way to the offices of Purdue, Hunt, and Pour, Lawyers. And twenty minutes after departing the law firm, he entered Maybell's, an establishment that was obviously the classiest whorehouse in Tucson.

Tallman settled on a bench across the street from the sex house, snatched a thin cheroot from his vest, stroked a sulphurhead on the weathered wooden seat, and fired up the expensive cigar. He figured that he would have time on his hands while Tucson's top politician got his goose strangled. He once again pondered his options, and became more convinced than ever that he would have to stretch the bounds of the law in order to assure the success of his mission.

Looking somehow drained, Westfall emerged from the whorehouse after only thirty minutes. The fat mayor looked into the high sun, adjusted his hat, hitched his pants, and proceeded west. After a ten-minute stroll he walked into the sheriff's office. Tallman followed and stopped at the edge of the window. Westfall was passing banknotes to the town's chief lawdog.

"Damn," Tallman whispered to himself as he moved away from the window. He had guessed that, with the exception of the stop at Maybell's, Westfall was making a payoff run. But what he had seen in the sheriff's office cinched it. The law would be of no use to him now. They would have to go it alone. He decided he would need Perry Oldham's cooperation. He also decided that they would have to move soon.

"After stopping in on the sheriff, the mayor went home," Tallman explained to Oldham. "And that's how I see it."

"So you think Westfall is the conduit for the payoffs?" the Wells Fargo division superintendent asked, after listening to the whole story. "Never thought that fellow had the intelligence or the nerve for anything like this."

"Looks like he must have, Perry. Of course, Traber probably has him scared stiff. He's probably threatened him with a one-way trip to the desert."

"Damn," Oldham grunted as he sat down. "But we still don't have anything on the stage robberies!" It was obvious he was steeping in his frustration.

"For all we know, Traber has nothing to do with it."

"We don't know for sure. But having watched Traber, I'm convinced that he would never pass up money as big as you have lost in the stickups. He's got his paws in everything around here. Even if he was not in on it at first, you can bet your last silver dollar that he's got a piece of the action now."

"Maybe so," Oldham sighed. He balled his fists; his huge muscles filled his white shirt. Though his body appeared as if it would explode, he spoke quietly. "I just keep thinking of my men. Four dead and one with his damn crotch all blown up."

"Tell you what!" Tallman said, his voice ringing with determination and finality. "Like I told you this morning, I think Traber is our man. I've been in this business a long time and I've seen plenty of Floyd Trabers. They have the law locked up, they cover tracks better than an Indian, and they usually feed a sacrificial lamb to the legal system on the rare occasion when they are caught. Let me stay on Traber tonight. If we don't learn anything more, I've got plans for Mayor Westfall. Something tells me that he is the weak link in the chain. Scared of his own shadow. I figure he'll sing the kind of tune we want to hear when he's given the alternatives I intend to offer him."

Oldham looked up from his desk. He smiled when he saw the look on Tallman's face.

THIRTEEN

Obie Stallybrass, the Buena Suerte floor manager, walked up to Vivian. "Jarrott wants to see you, Susanna," he said, shrugging his slumped shoulders. "He and Floyd Traber just went upstairs."

"I saw them, Obie," Vivian said to the congenial man. "Wonder what Sherm's got up his sleeve now."

Obie shrugged again and walked off to get another dealer for her table. Vivian got up, her senses heightened by the prospect that she might somehow once again have the opportunity to worm her way in on Traber's operation. She knew she could get hurt toying with a rattlesnake, but she was becoming more determined as the case appeared to be at a standstill. This was her chance to crack it wide open.

Tallman, still sporting his Cyrus Purdy getup, popped through the Buena Suerte doors just as Vivian was making her way to the stairs. Their eyes locked for an instant, but neither missed a stride.

The mining speculator ordered whiskey just as Vivian knocked on the center balcony door.

"Who is it?" Jarrott asked.

"Susanna."

"Oh. Come in."

"Obie said you wanted to see me, Sherm," she said as she walked in, thrusting her breasts forward and setting her eyes in her best bedroom gaze.

"I asked Sherm to invite you up," Traber butted in, his blue eyes twinkling through narrow slits. His deep, long wrinkles and the long, thick gray mustache made him look the part of a villain in a cheap theater production. "I'd like to have you join me for dinner. I've got—"

"Floyd," Jarrott interrupted. "It's going to cost me a bundle to lose Susanna again tonight."

"You can afford it," Traber said, his calm and jesting voice in contrast with his evil eyes.

"Jesus Christ!"

"Gentlemen! I *do* earn my living dealing. Maybe we could make it another time, Mr. Traber. Perhaps my night off." Vivian said, hoping to show loyalty toward Jarrott. She knew Traber would not back down anyhow.

"Nonsense, Susanna!" Traber said, his wrinkles creased deeper than usual. "This charlatan can switch your night off."

"Go ahead, Susanna," Jarrott said, wishing that he had the nerve to kill Traber and take over Tucson. "That is, if you want to."

"Well, I'm . . . of course I'm flattered!"

"It's settled, then," Traber said as he slapped his palms on the arms of the chair and stood up.

Vivian faked a sheepish look toward Jarrott and accepted Traber's bony hand.

On the way out of the casino, Vivian stopped for her wrap and shot Tallman an apprehensive look just as Hall left the bar to join her and the vice czar.

Tallman understood.

"You fascinate me, Floyd," Vivian said as she sipped the champagne the waiter had just poured from the second expensive bottle. She wondered how the French bubbly ever made it to Tucson. "I've always been attracted to men who know where they are going and how to get there."

"A fine compliment, Susanna. I like your style," Traber responded with raised eyebrows, as he flicked the ash from his cigar into his empty dinner platter. "Something tells me there is more to Susanna Duncan than meets the eye."

Vivian flinched at the words, but quickly recovered.

"I mean," Traber said when he noticed her momentary discomfort. "There is a mind to go with your other charms. Charms which are numerous," he added. "Your intelligence, I gather, is a little something you keep hidden for your own purposes. Something like a hideout gun. Very bright of you.

My mother was brilliant," he said, an odd trace of fear flashing in his eyes. "Intelligence and looks. Often an elusive combination in a woman."

Vivian nodded and sipped champagne, wondering what his mother had to do with it. She'd find out soon enough.

"Well," Traber went on. "It would be a shame to end the evening so early. Would you care to join me at my house for an after-dinner drink?" Traber tightened his horizontal forehead wrinkles as he awaited an answer.

Knowing looks passed across the white tablecloth, which contained the remnants of the best steak dinner in Tucson. Traber knew Vivian would accept the invitation to his bed only because he had the potential to advance her position in the world, and it showed in his eyes. And Vivian's eyes revealed that she knew what he knew.

"I'd love to, Floyd."

Several minutes later they left the restaurant and, to Vivian's distress, a half bottle of rare champagne. With the tree-stump bodyguard at the reins, they rode at a brisk trot toward the vice czar's home. Shortly, Hall pulled up the matched chestnuts in front of the vice lord's expensively appointed residence. Once in the house, he poured French brandy into two crystal glasses that rested elegantly on an ornately carved walnut bar. His taste was impeccable, and, so far, his deportment had been gentlemanly.

"Judd, you may go now," Traber said to his gorilla

after Hall had put a match to the lamps in the parlor and bedroom.

Then Traber stood looking at the lady blackjack dealer with an odd expression in his eyes. For an instant, Vivian thought he looked like a little boy. "Let's retire to the bedroom," he said bluntly, his strange look growing in intensity.

Vivian let her lips smile ever so slightly, took hold of his knobby fingers, and urged him down the hallway.

FOURTEEN

Tallman, concealed in a row of scrub pines that marked the boundary of Traber's property, was concerned by the noises coming from the dimly lit back room. Once, he'd been tempted to charge the place, but he resisted his jealous impulse, trusting Vivian. And the dog-faced Judd Hall sat quietly on the porch burning one cigarette after another.

Nonetheless, the thought of Vivian and Traber together left him uneasy. He told himself it wasn't jealousy or the thought that Vivian might have to let Traber sample her luscious fruits. He was simply concerned for her safety. Friends were hard to come by. And the longer they worked together, the more respect he gained for the long-legged woman who was as willing to chomp off big slices of life and swallow them whole as he was. He sensed that an ironclad friendship was slowly being riveted in place.

While he was pondering this possibility and

shifting his position, a man walked up the street and deliberately and quickly turned into Traber's small yard.

"Hoped I'd find you here, Judd," the man said, his voice showing respect for Hall.

"Quiet! The boss is busy."

Both men laughed aloud, then abruptly silenced themselves.

"Let's go into the carriage house," Hall muttered. "Don't want to bother the boss."

Both men walked toward the other side of the house, their conversation turning into a jumble of sounds.

Acutely aware of the bright moon and the still air, Tallman quietly worked his way around the back of the small barn. Despite his new vantage point, the voices were still mumbles intertwined with sinister laughter.

After ten minutes of incomprehensible jabbering, the visitor shook Hall's hand and walked toward the street. Tallman, faced with a dilemma, decided to tail the stranger, allowing that Vivian could take care of herself.

For half a mile, Tallman followed the stranger through the distinct shadows cast by the brilliant moon. As the man turned and walked a narrow path to a small frame house, Tallman carefully noted the location and hurried back to Traber's extravagant home. As he cut across a neighbor's lot and made a beeline for the hedge, he saw the red glow of Hall's cigarette. Things seemed unchanged.

Tallman was shifting his position to ease the cramp in his side from his cross-draw rig and to ease the pain in his back, which came from his being hunched up in the pine hedge for the past hour and a half since he'd returned from tailing the stranger. He had just settled into a better position when he heard Traber.

"Judd!"

He looked up and saw the tree-stump henchman open the front door. Minutes later, Vivian, Traber, and the bodyguard stepped onto the porch.

Their words were clear in the still night air.

"See Susanna home, will you, Judd."

"Sure, boss," Hall said, before turning to go for the carriage.

Once the guard rounded the corner of the house, Vivian and Traber spoke quietly as she hung onto his arm as if she'd found her first schoolyard sweetheart. Tallman chuckled to himself and shook his bowler-topped head in awe, thankful that Vivian was on his side. And, truth be known, he was relieved to know that she was safe and still in pursuit.

When Hall wheeled out of the carriage house and stopped at the porch steps, Traber helped Vivian aboard.

"Boss," Hall said in his gruff voice. "We had a visitor tonight while you was—ah—entertain'."

"Yes?"

"Our friend in the shippin' business. Says he's got work for us to tend to, day after tomorrow."

"I'll keep it in mind," Traber said calmly. "No need to bore Miss Duncan with business."

Tallman smiled, feeling confident that the man he had tailed across town was the final link. He was also amused at the tone of reprimand in Traber's voice. Hall would hear about his indiscretion in front of Vivian.

"Sure, boss," Hall responded, his tone sheepish.

"Oh, my! You do stay busy," Vivian chimed in. "Here it is the wee hours of the morning and you're still doing business."

"Staying on top is a full-time job, Susanna," Traber allowed, as the horses snorted and shifted in the cool night air. "The bigger beasts eat the smaller ones and so on."

"Well, Floyd, if I can ever be of any help, you know where I am."

Tallman heard no reply.

"I'll stop by the Buena Suerte on the way back. Talk to Sherm," Hall went on. "It will save a trip."

"Good idea, Judd. I'll see you in half an hour."

Hall slapped the reins on the matched chestnuts, and the well-schooled horses stepped into an organized trot, their white stockings flashing in the moonlight.

• • •

As Tallman entered his room in the Governor, he scaled the bowler across the room to his bed, stripped off the mustache, and loosened his stiff white collar. His back was still slightly cramped and he was beginning to feel a sense of urgency. On the walk back to the hotel, he had decided that he would force the gang's hand, one way or another. He would follow the stranger in the morning, and if that led up a blind alley, he'd decided to squeeze Tucson's blubbery mayor until something came out. But he had a feeling that the mysterious business Hall had mentioned was another stage job for Doc and his strange mama. It fitted what Pearl had said before the last job.

Tallman rubbed the excess spirit gum off his upper lip and then dipped a towel in the basin of fresh water. After he had rubbed his neck and face clean, he slumped in the overstuffed chair in the corner of the hotel room and broke out a cheroot. He wanted to wait an hour before seeing Vivian. And if he went to sleep, he knew it would be for more than an hour.

"Thought you would never show, Ash," Vivian whispered as she let her fellow Pinkerton into her room.

"I wanted to let the dust settle," he answered quietly. "After what happened the other night, I wanted to wait and then take a careful look around before coming here."

Vivian walked toward the tall, sandy-haired detective, locked her fingers behind his neck and pulled him to her lips. She probed urgently with her tongue and literally shuddered with desire.

Tallman put his hand on her hips and felt velvet skin, slippery under the maroon-and-black silk lace nightgown.

Tallman backed away and raised his right eyebrow. "You've got that look in your eye, Viv," he kidded. "I'd have thought three hours with old Floyd would have tuckered you out!"

"Me? Tuckered out? You men are the ones with the limitations. Us ladies can go as long as it suits our fancy!" she exclaimed, with a twinkle of lust in her green eyes, as she spun away and walked toward the bed. Her hips moved under silk in a way that would cause a man's heart to skip a beat. She sat on the goosedown and looked right at her lithe, steely-eyed partner. "Truth is, Traber has nothing to offer. Remind me to tell you about it some time when I get up my courage and when you are up for a moment of tearful laughter."

"Sounds interesting," Tallman said as he walked toward her dresser. "Where did you get this?" he asked as he looked at the bottle of French brandy. "Allan will choke when he sees this on the expense report!"

"A gift from Sherm."

"*Sherm,* is it!" he said as he poured some of the amber liquid into one of the crystal glasses that rested next to the brandy. "God have mercy on Vivian Valentine's men!"

"Were you with me tonight?" she asked, bringing the conversation back to business.

"Cyrus Purdy was sneaking about in the bushes all night," he replied after sniffing his glass. "Matter of fact, I've been sneaking about since early this morning. But nothing more came of it until this evening. That is, with the exception of the restaurant I discovered this morning. After we clean this up, I insist that we have breakfast there."

"Hall's visitor?" Vivian asked. "Your success this evening?"

"Very observant, Miss Valentine," he said, his mood mellowing, his voice becoming sonorous. "I suspect that we have a line to our Judas. While you were engaged . . . in whatever . . . with your gray-haired beanstalk, I tailed the messenger to his little home across town. And I'll be up with the roosters to see how the man fits into the organization." Tallman swirled the cognac in his snifter as he went to the corner chair, which was identical to the one in his room. "Traber is definitely running the local protection racket. I followed him today as he made his rounds. Also I snaked after that lard-assed politician, Westfall. He made the rounds too. It's obvious that he is their lackey. He came out of Traber's real-estate office with a fist full of banknotes in a white envelope. At least that's my guess. I don't think it was a love letter."

"You might think different if I ever get around to telling you about our vice lord," Vivian said, a note of disgust in her voice.

Tallman allowed Vivian a wry smile after another taste of the cognac. "Not much more to tell . . . except that Westfall visited the sheriff and passed on a handful of banknotes. I guess it stands to reason that they need his cooperation to keep the owners of the saloons, gaming joints, and whorehouses in line."

"But other than the possibility that the Hall's visitor is the missing link, we need more to connect Traber and Pearl Bowen."

"That's a fact . . . if you are talking courtroom requirements." His tone was cool, utterly assured. "But tomorrow will tell. If Traber's visitor leads nowhere, I'm going to squeeze Westfall until he squirts. I have a feeling that he will give."

"I agree," Vivian said as she fluffed the large pillow at the head of the wide bed. When she slapped at the pillow, her firm breasts, nipples extended, moved under the low-cut maroon silk. "The others are sharp," she said matter-of-factly as she flopped supine. "Westfall is a real shitbird!"

Tallman, settled by the taste of the French brandy and the magical sight on the bed, got up, slipped off his jacket, hideout rig, and vest, and walked to the bed. "That wheatstalk didn't give you any incurable diseases, did he?" Tallman kidded as he set the snifter on the bedside table.

"Not unless you can catch something off the handle of a cat-o'-nine-tails!" Vivian laughed, quickly checking the loud howl by burying her face in the pillow.

"One of those?"

"Yep," she whispered. "The only way he could get it up was if I beat the shit out of him." She giggled, her green eyes flashing her rare zest for life. "And I have to tell you," she went on like a little kid talking of ghosts. "I'm plumb tuckered out."

Vivian leaned toward the small table and took his glass.

"I gather you didn't learn anything," Tallman went on as he unlaced his shoes. He knew she would have told him right off if she had.

"No. I tried to snake something out of him, but he shut me off each time. I know when to stop."

Vivian sipped the cognac from his glass as he put his trousers over the chair. His manhood had grown stiff in his drawers. As his partner lay there, she seemed to have a faint aura about her brushed auburn hair. Supported on one elbow, her ample breasts sloped, ever so slightly, down and away. She glowed under the kerosene light, her bare arms, lissome calves, and her face all in a sensual contrast with the maroon nightgown.

She set down the glass and reached for the lump

in his shorts. "What's this," she asked as she gripped the oblong shape in his underwear. "And what's that look in your eyes?"

"That thing in your hand is a three-hour erection that's as hard as a railroad spike. And you see hunger in my eyes. The same horrible curse left upon us all by an angry God!"

"Thank goodness Adam and Eve took the temptation," she said, her eyes fixed on his, her hands jerking down his drawers. "God's anger is now my pleasure."

Tallman stepped out of his shorts and settled in the goosedown. He rolled toward her and sought her lips with his as she reached for his cock and began to finger the swollen tip. He sucked her tongue into his mouth and cupped one cheek of her firm ass with his strong hand, his fingertips on the very edge of her opening. The feel of the flesh under the silk heightened his senses, and he pulled aside the nightgown, pushed one leg aside, and grabbed her damp crotch firmly. Slowly, he moved three fingers up and down the slick, pink meat between her throbbing lips. Once again, Tallman pondered her wetness as he had done many times before. Though he had sampled the fruit of many women, none got as wet as Vivian. He slipped his middle finger into her as she arched her back and drew her feet up to her buttocks and opened her legs wide.

"Harder, Ash!"

Tallman drove his finger deeper and pressed on the curls above the opening with his thumb.

She broke the kiss and sought his ear with her darting tongue. Tallman tightened his hold as he pulled down her thin straps and exposed a breast. Vivian began bucking against his hand as he latched onto her nipple with feverish abandon.

"Ooooo, Ash! God-I-love-to-fuck," she groaned. Her speech was more guttural sounds than words. A rhythmic surging grew in her groin as he sucked loudly on her breast. She put a hand in his sandy hair and pushed him firmly against her breast as she flicked the bloodred tip of his cock with her other hand. Her hips moved faster. Her sounds became more primitive.

Then, in one lurching move, she dropped his cock, pulled away from his sucking, rolled over, and got to her knees. "Stick it in . . . *fast!* Fuck me *hard!*" she moaned, always aware of the effect such talk had on a man.

She dropped her face to the pillow and arched her back, exposing an oblong patch of hair that was matted with dampness. He got to his knees and inched forward, his thick shaft arching for relief. Once he had his knees between hers, he ran the swollow head of his cock up and down her slit, savoring her wetness.

"Ahhhhh. Jesus! Assssh!" she groaned as she tried to back on to him. "Fuck me!"

Tallman obliged. He stopped at her hole and bucked violently forward, driving his rod to the bottom of her hot cunt. Then he leaned over her and grabbed her tits out of the loose silk and began to twirl the hard nipples. Slowly, he pulled back and forth as her secretions flowed down his balls. Vivian moved her hand to the top of her womanhood, resting on her shoulder and one arm. While he pumped her wet cunt and fondled her hanging tits, she fingered her love button. Both were lost. Reality abandoned, they moved like a locomotive with four drivewheels, pistons throbbing, wheels spinning in perfect synchronization, steam hissing, connecting rods thumping.

"Fuck me!" she grunted as waves of pleasure began to overcome her.

Tallman held her tits and pumped with superhuman speed as he felt the first tingling spasm.

"Ahhhh. Oh! Oh, Ash!" she grunted between rapid breaths.

Oblivious of any other occurrence in the world, they tangled in final blows, Tallman gushing pent-up seed, Vivian releasing a flood of juice. Shuddering in unison, they pushed toward the final wave; then they slept.

FIFTEEN

As Tallman paced under the gray morning sky, he swore to himself that he would go to his Chicago hideaway after the pending Wells Fargo job and sleep for three days straight. His eyes were sore from a lack of shuteye and he longed for a steaming cup of coffee. Vivid images of his one decent breakfast at the Poste y Dehesa restaurant broke the morning's boredom and caused his stomach to rumble. He'd been staked out near the house of the messenger for over an hour. Tallman looked toward the mountains and smiled. He reached inside his plain but carefully constructed rawhide jacket and snatched a thin cigar from his blue cotton shirt. Since he had decided to force the action in the case, he had discarded Cyrus Purdy in favor of his comfortable Levis, well-worn expensive boots, tailored shirt, and flat-brim Stetson.

He fired up the cheroot and looked toward the house of the stranger. Nothing. He flipped the match on to the damp earth, snugged his Stetson, adjusted the side holster he'd put on in place of his concealed rig, and resumed his pacing.

As the gray sky began to turn light blue, the residential street began to stir. Then, shortly after the warm rays of the sun broke over Eagle Peak, the man who had visited the bent-nosed Judd Hall the night before emerged from his little house. Tallman carefully noted the man's clothing and hat and stayed well away from the unsuspecting stranger. After a short walk past plain women shaking carpets, slashing walks with brooms, and shouting kids off to school, the messenger turned on to Commercial Street. Tallman moved closer to his mark, as the business district was already teeming with activity. Two blocks north on the Commercial plank-walk, the man stopped, turned, and entered a familiar door.

Tallman stopped dead in his tracks, shook his head, and beamed a broad smile. Oldham's problem was about to be solved.

The man had walked right into the Wells Fargo office.

Tallman lifted and reseated his Stetson and strolled into the office.

"Mr. Oldham in?" he asked the stranger, who was just hanging his coat on a wooden peg.

"No doubt," the young Judas answered. "Usually the first one here and the last one to leave. Figure he loves this place more than life itself."

Tallman caught a sour note in the man's voice.

"What's your name, mister?" Tallman asked the blond-haired young man.

"Billy Harkins. Express clerk."

"Ash Tallman, Pinkerton agent," he said, his eyes fixed on the man's questioning gaze as he slowly unholstered his Colt, thumbed the hammer, and put cold steel right on the clerk's forehead. One of the other employees gasped. Then the office went still. "Billy," Tallman went on. "What say you and I go talk to Mr. Oldham about stage robbery and murder."

"Damn," someone moaned.

"Let's go, Billy," he said as he pressed the barrel tighter to the express clerk's forehead. "And I want the rest of you to stay put. No one leaves this office. And no one says a thing. Otherwise you'll be up on charges. Conspiracy to commit murder."

The clerk backed slowly toward Oldham's door as Tallman kept the Colt's muzzle pressed to his pale skin. The Judas was frightened white.

"What the hell's—" Oldham stammered as the pair came into his office. "What the hell are you—"

"Thought you might like a few words with Judas reincarnated before I got to work on him," Tallman said in a monotone. "Might not be much left of this slime by the time I'm finished."

"Jesus Christ . . . Billy," Oldham wheezed. "Why?"

"I don't know what he is talking about," the clerk spat, his voice cracking. "He's crazy!"

"I caught him passing information on tomorrow's shipment."

Oldham sighed. Tallman had not known of the shipment.

"He told Judd Hall and Traber. And Hall then went right to Jarrott. And we know Jarrott is linked to Pearl Bowen and her cutthroats. Case is all but locked up," he added, hoping to set the clerk up to squeal all he knew.

"You son-of-a-bitch," Oldham shouted as he grabbed the clerk by the collar. His face went purple as he twisted the man's shirt tight against his Adam's apple and lifted him to his toes. "We've lost four good men, had two passengers killed, two women raped, and Wes Herman is over at Doc Alexander's, gutshot and missin' two balls!"

"But I didn't—"

"Shut up, you scum!" Tallman said as he pushed Oldham off and put his Colt in its leather. "Keep your goddamned mouth shut and listen. You are likely going to hang with the whole town lookin' on. We have you cold, son." Tallman knew that they needed more than they had to lock up Jarrott and Traber. But he was hoping to turn the express clerk on the others. "But there is an outside chance we might be able to persuade the judge to let you live if you cut the bullshit and come straight with us."

Harkins, seeing the Pinkerton's gun holstered, darted for the open door. Tallman, expecting a move like that, swung on the willowy clerk, catching him between the shoulder blades with his right fist. With a thump and a whoosh of air, the man sprawled forward and skidded across the wooden floor on his face. Tallman walked over, picked the clerk up by his belt, and jerked him into a chair. Then the Judas began to sob, his shoulders bucking forward, bloody snot dripping from his scraped nose.

"All I did was tell 'em when," he sobbed. "I never killed nobody."

"You goddamned—you—you bastard! You might as well have killed them yourself," Oldham shouted.

"Cool down, Perry," Tallman broke in.

"Jesus. To think of Wes," Oldham mumbled as he went to his desk.

"Go on, Billy," he urged, affecting a fatherly voice.

"They gave me five hundred dollars each time. That's all. I just told Judd Hall when, and they paid me."

"Goddamn!" Oldham shouted. "Five hundred dollars! You sold out four of the people you worked with for five hundred dollars!"

"That's right!" the clerk spat. His whimpering suddenly turned to rage. "A man can't live on what you pay. Fuckin' Wells Fargo. You and the bankers, the railroads, the shopkeepers, and the politicians. Break a man's back and throw him away. My old man died laying rails, and they barely took time to bury the poor old son-of-a-bitch. Fuck all of you!"

Oldham got out of his chair, his arms tense, his fists balled the size of small melons. The barrel-chested district superintendent could have killed the spindly clerk with one blow. Oldham's eyes were burning embers.

"Perry! Relax. You'll get your satisfaction when he falls through the scaffolding."

Oldham slumped back into his chair and slammed his fist on his cluttered desk, causing a large wind-up clock to jump to the floor.

"Stand up, Harkins," Tallman ordered as he jerked the clerk out of the chair. He was now angry with the Judas after hearing the man's little speech. Tallman had always believed that each man has control of life until the end, and that whimpering malcontents like Harkins were the curse of the earth, the pawns of vain politicians who rode to power on class-struggle rhetoric. They were, in his mind, evil men without even knowing it. And, in *his* mind, that made them more dangerous than any two Doc Strouds. "So you got it all figured out, Billy?" Tallman said as he undid the man's belt and jerked it off. "Everybody in the world who ever got anywhere is the reason you're nobody." He tied the clerk's hands behind his back. "People have been singing that tune since the beginning of time, my friend." He pushed the clerk back into the chair. "And it got them just about as far as it's going to get you," he went on, as he pulled his five-inch boot knife and sliced the sleeve off the man's shirt. "One-way fare to Hell, boy," Tallman said as he gagged the Judas with his severed shirt sleeve.

He turned to Oldham. "That a closet?"

"Yeah."

He grabbed the chair by its back and dragged the clerk and the chair into the closet. With the door still open, he asked Oldham if he could trust the district manager not to kill Harkins. He was only *half* kidding. Oldham was obviously enraged over the fate of his friend, Wes Herman.

"I have a mind to take his nuts," Oldham answered.

"Leave his nuts," Tallman said. "Just tap him in the head if he gives you any trouble . . . lightly."

He slammed the closet door and whispered to Oldham. Tallman explained that if any word of Harkins's confinement went beyond the office, they would lose the case and likely stand before the judge themselves. When Oldham suggested that they inform the law, Tallman reminded him of the trip Westfall made to the sheriff's office. The Wells Fargo man got the message.

Once in the outer office, Tallman warned the employees that one word of the morning's events would ruin their chances of capturing the outlaws and thus make the loose-lipped offender a party to the crime.

"I'll go one further," Oldham growled. "I've lost a couple of friends. And Wes Herman and I go twenty years back when we rode shotgun together. Any of you mess this up and I guarantee that you will not even make it to prison," he went on as he put his hand on his small sidearm. "That clear?"

The nine people in the office understood perfectly, and it was obvious that most were eager to help.

"Let's take a walk," Tallman said, after carefully making eye-contact with each of the Wells Fargo employees.

Outside, he explained that he wanted someone to explain to Harkins's wife that he'd been sent to San Manuel on business. He further explained that he wanted Pearl alive so that they could use her to break Jarrott.

"Then we'll use Pearl, Jarrott, and Harkins to nail Traber and Hall. We'll offer them a deal to testify against Traber. And believe me, we'll need it. Something tells me Traber is more deeply entrenched in Territorial politics than we know. We will need everything we can get to make him walk the scaffold."

"Those three *should* be enough."

"No," Tallman said as he bit the tip of a fresh cheroot. "I want insurance."

"Insurance?"

"Westfall."

Tallman waited in the shadows on the plankwalk across from the Buena Suerte. The street was alive with drunks, loud and on the lookout for a one-dollar piece of ass. The banjo, the bass, and the piano hammered out a lively tune, which easily rang beyond the stained-glass doors of Jarrott's gaming joint. Westfall had been inside for two hours.

Finally, just after ten o'clock, the fat mayor waddled out of the jack-of-spades door. He hadn't gone ten feet when he began jawing and backslapping with every other drunk he met on the boardwalk.

"Goddamn politicians," Tallman muttered under his breath. "God's own personal joke on mankind." He had been on Westfall's tail for some time, hoping to find him alone, even though most glad-handed public officials were never alone.

But, to his distress, it was more of the same. It took the politician a half hour to go three blocks to his next stop, Novak's Dance Hall, an obvious whorehouse.

As Westfall entered the pleasure house, Tallman slumped into a bench across the street and lit a cigar. One skill a good Pinkerton had to master was waiting.

Shortly after midnight, Westfall emerged from Novak's. The streets had quieted some, as many of the locals had gone home to nagging wives. Only the hardcore drunks and gamblers remained. For them, the evening was just beginning.

After Westfall thumped along for two blocks, Tallman saw his first opportunity of the evening. He snatched his boot knife, surveyed the street quickly, and dashed the ten yards separating him from the mayor. He grabbed Westfall's sleeve and flung him into the alley.

"One word, fat man, and I push a little harder," he growled as he held the razor-sharp knife to Westfall's throat, nicking the skin just hard enough to start a trickle of blood.

"Jesus, mister," Westfall wheezed. "Take my money and my watch but *please* don't hurt me! *Please!*"

"You are going to lose more than your watch unless you do just as I say. Now . . . let's walk very slowly to the Wells Fargo office," Tallman said, as he took the knife from Westfall's neck and pressed the point into the fat man's side. "One false move and I'll slip this little baby into your heart so quick you won't have time to say the first three words of the Lord's Prayer."

Without incident, they made their way to Oldham's office. Westfall had kept up a steady stream of cowardly pleading all the while.

"What the hell is going on?" Westfall said when he saw Oldham. "What do you think you are doing?"

The mayor was a sorry sight under the dim kerosene light.

"What we are doing," Tallman broke in, "is implicating you in murder, robbery, and mail tampering. Put simply mister, you're in deep shit."

"Who the hell are you?" Westfall asked, his voice slightly bolder.

"Ashley Tallman. Pinkerton Agency."

"Pinkertons!" His voice sagged with his shoulders. No criminal ever wanted to hear those words.

"Listen up, Westfall. We've got several agents in your operation," he lied.

"Operation!"

"I said listen, partner. We've got enough on you, Traber, Jarrott, and the others to send the bunch of you dancing through the trapdoor."

As Tallman provided the mayor with details, the politician's chubby pink lips sagged with his jowls and heavy eyelids. While the Pinkerton deftly manipulated the mayor into thinking that all was lost, Oldham sat behind his desk glaring at Westfall.

"But you can't take the law into your own hands. Let's take this up with the sheriff," Westfall whined. "He's the law. You're not."

"Westfall, he's as crooked as you." With that, Tallman drew his Colt and put the large bore muzzle right on the tip of the mayor's red-veined nose. "Sheriff's not going to hear about anything. And I'm tired of wasting time with you. I've been short on sleep lately and I'm a might cranky. So start talking or say goodbye."

"I'm no good to you dead!" Westfall pleaded in a quaking voice. His forehead was damp with cold sweat. "You—you—ca—can't get away with this," he stammered.

"It's easy, mister," Tallman said as he thumbed back the hammer on the Colt. "I'll shoot you right here and now and we'll crate you up and ship you out on the morning freighter. All compliments of Wells Fargo. Now . . . You've got ten seconds."

Westfall promptly assessed Tallman's determination and willingness to send him on his final journey to Hell. In ten minutes the hog-jowled Tucson mayor had outlined what he knew about Traber's activities. He explained that, although he had no specific knowledge of the stage robberies, he had assumed that Traber had a hand in it. From the brief sketch given by the frightened politician, they discovered that the ring's operations extended well beyond stage robbery and vice-district extortion. Westfall claimed to have knowledge of fraudulent contracts with the Army and Indian reservation agents and of crooked land deals.

When Westfall was done squealing on his associates, Oldham and Tallman bound the man to a chair, gagged him with a dustrag, and skidded the hulk into the closet with Harkins, the latter being no small task.

"How are you fixed for sleep?" Tallman asked Oldham. "Can you watch these two jackals tonight?"

Oldham smiled and nodded as he lifted a short-barreled twelve-gauge from behind his desk, cracked it, and dropped in two loads of buckshot.

"Shoot the bastards if you have to," Tallman said loudly for the benefit of the duo in the closet. "They are both killers just the same as if they personally shot your guards."

"I'd fancy an excuse to send these bums to Hell. One of them for each of Wes Herman's nuts. Hardly a fair trade, but it would be a start!"

"I'll be back before sunrise, Perry," Tallman went on. "I want to brief my partner and think through a couple of details on a plan I've got cooking. Send your night clerk out to round up four of your best men. Have them here by six."

Oldham nodded.

"I think we'll send out a shipment on the nine o'clock stage that Pearl and her bunch will find very costly," Tallman said with a wry smile as he ran his fingers through his sandy-colored hair. Then the detective seated his Stetson and headed into the chilly night air.

SIXTEEN

As Tallman made his way to the Wells Fargo office, the sky was threatening rain. Low gray scud swirled overhead, blocking any sign of the rising sun.

"Gentlemen," Tallman said as he entered the office and found Perry Oldham and four other men milling about with coffee cups hanging from their fingers. Then a trace of a thin smile appeared on his lips. "Looks like a nice day for a funeral."

"Damned if it ain't," one of the men chortled, while the others vented nervous laughter.

Oldham quickly but proudly introduced the four express guards. Two were dressed as whiskey drummers, one wore a storekeeper's get-up, and the tallest of the bunch looked like any Wells Fargo guard or driver. "All of them capable . . . and every one of them a friend of Wes Herman."

"I'm hopin' we cut somebody's nuts today," the tallest of the bunch grunted.

"The one we're after doesn't have any nuts," Tallman said as he stared at the tall guard. "The one we want has tits. And we want her *alive*."

"Tits!" the guard shot back.

"Tits." Tallman confirmed. "Her name's Pearl Bowen. And she's the most deadly of the bunch."

"Was it her who gutshot Wes and took target practice on his nuts?"

Tallman gave the express guard an affirmative nod.

"Dogshit!" he wheezed.

"I gather Perry's briefed you boys on what you're here for," Tallman went on in a serious tone. "That pisswillie tied up in the back room has been selling you out. I'm damn near positive that he squawked the night before last about the nine o'clock stage this morning. You were scheduled to carry thirty-one thousand in gold and silver. It's the kind of thing they couldn't pass up."

Tallman continued to brief the men on what he expected of them. He finally explained that he wanted three of them to leave the Wells Fargo office as inconspicuously as possible and ride to the relay station on the outskirts of Pantano. "Just on the outside chance they got someone watching here in Tucson."

After the men had left, Tallman told Oldham he wanted him to continue to stand watch on the mayor and the express clerk.

An hour and a half after the three riders had departed, the stage rumbled to a stop in front of the

Tucson depot. The team stood quietly as the driver, the large, vocal express guard, and Tallman threw aboard five empty bags and an empty oak-and-brass strongbox.

"You ride shotgun," Tallman said to the tall, mean-looking guard he'd held back. "I'll go inside."

At exactly nine, the stage pulled away with its one passenger, the driver and the guard. The air was still and the black-bottomed clouds cast an eerie darkness on the barren countryside. The high-wheel coach jolted and swayed over the rutted road as the team snorted and strained against collars, chains, and the iron hitch. Tallman pondered the likelihood of getting himself and the four express guards out alive. Pearl and her gang would have the edge, even though *they* had surprise on their side. He looked out the window, shook his head, and settled back in the leather seat. He wanted Pearl alive, and he knew that might be costly.

In just under two hours, the driver hauled the horses up at the Pantano way station. Inside, the stationkeeper and the three guards were just finishing fried eggs, chili, and coffee.

"See you boys made it," Tallman said after he walked into the spartan cabin. He poured coffee into a tin cup and sat at the long wooden table just as the stationkeeper got up to go outside to change the team.

"Listen in!" he started. "Here's how we're going

to organize this turkey shoot. You," he said, pointing to the tall guard who'd ridden shotgun on the way from Tucson. "You'll be on top with the driver. I'll be inside with you three." He paused, pointing at each one of them, allowing his eyes to caution each man about the potential danger in the ambush. "Now, get this straight. I want the woman alive. I don't give a shit if the other three die screaming. But we need the bitch to get the higher-ups to the gallows."

The men listened carefully, taken with Tallman's direct and serious tone.

"Don't *any* of you take any chances! Doc Stroud, Jake, and Kirk would each one shoot their own brothers for six bits. *Don't* under any circumstances let one of these nasty belly-crawlers get the edge on you."

Tallman slowly turned his head, again looking into the eyes of each man. "You all carrying shotguns and Colts like Perry asked?"

They nodded.

"Double-O-buck?"

Their heads bobbed again.

"We don't know where we'll get it. But you can bet your ass they'll pick a spot that will make it tough on us."

"What about the cunt?" the tall guard grunted. "Who takes her?"

"I'll get to her," Tallman said, as he paused to nip the end off a thin cigar. "But first, I want to explain how I expect them to hit us."

Tallman went on with a detailed explanation of how the gang had pulled the holdup a week before. Then, after he'd given a description of Pearl, he asked the driver and the four others each to repeat what he'd said.

"Good," he said as he scratched a match on the tabletop and lit the cheroot. "We leave in ten minutes."

In just over an hour, they had passed Mescal without incident and started into the north edge of the Whetstone Mountains. Though the rain had held off, the air felt damp. They climbed a straight trail that Mother Nature had carved into the barren foothills. The drop-offs on the left were becoming more severe as the horses' slow and steady trot took them east.

Tallman was becoming more at ease as he watched the men. None looked overly apprehensive or offered nervous babble. Each was quiet and keen-eyed.

But moments later, Tallman's senses were piqued when the driver snapped the reins as they began to climb a steeper grade. The horses snorted and pulled harder, but the coach slowed. Then he heard Doc's voice.

"Hold that team, Mister—or die!"

The driver halted as they'd planned. As before, Jake and Kirk came from behind. At once, Tallman saw Pearl up on a rock to his left, her Winchester sighted on the guard. Then Kirk opened the door.

"Hoodoo! What the—"

The twelve-gauge cradled by the guard next to Tallman exploded, sending sixteen lead balls into Kirk's chest and face. The outlaw bucked backward in a red mist of bone and meat and thumped to the ground just as Pearl fired on the guard. The tall express guard was jolted from the seat by the impact of Pearl's forty-four rifle slug. When he hit the ground head-first, he was dead, half his brain hanging from the gap in his skull.

The air was instantly thick with shotgun explosions, pistol fire, and the sounds of spooked horses. The men scrambled, firing as they emerged from the high-wheeled coach. One of the guards stitched three forty-five pistol slugs up Jake's vest, each one causing the stage robber to dance backward until his legs turned to rubber, and he fell in a twisted, twitching heap.

Doc was still firing his pistol when the stage driver, struggling with the reins in his left hand, fired both barrels of his shotgun with the other hand. Most of the pellets kicked up the hardpan dirt behind Doc and to his left, but two stray lead bullets caught his left arm, spinning him to the ground.

As Doc scrambled for cover, Pearl loosed two more shots at the driver. Both missed as the stage lurched and jolted at the frantic beckon of the terror-stricken horses.

Pearl, seeing that she'd been outfoxed and outgunned, ducked and sprinted for her horse. Tallman saw her disappear and, after calling for the men to cease firing, he scrambled up the rocks toward the spot he'd last seen her. As he got to the top, he saw Doc and Pearl racing away in a full gallop. Seeing she was going to get away, Tallman took a careful bead on her horse and fired. He saw a spot of red appear on the meaty part of the horse's shoulder, but Pearl was out of pistol range before he could shoot again. Encouraged by the fact that Pearl's horse was hit and by the realization that Doc was trailing a bum arm, he sprinted for Jake's dappled gray, mounted, and kicked the horse after the outlaws.

Pearl pulled up to Doc, who was squirting blood out of his lower arm. His wrist was shattered.

"You all right?" Pearl shouted over the sounds of the frantic horses.

He shook his head, his white face wrinkled with pain and fear.

They held the pace for several minutes, but Pearl's horse slowed despite her savage kicking.

"Over there," she shouted when she spotted a trail which led to a small ridge. She had a plan.

When they cleared the ridge, Pearl dismounted and slapped a fresh round into her Winchester. Doc grunted as he slid from his sticky saddle, stumbled, and went down on his ass.

Pearl fell prone on the crest of the ridge and aimed her rifle at the oncoming rider.

Tallman heard the whine of the slow and heavy slug as it passed. Just as he heard the rifle's report he reined his horse left, then right, while he scanned the ground ahead. Seeing the ridge, he made a zigzag dash toward a grove of scrubby evergreens.

Doc, who had crawled over the ridge twenty feet to Pearl's left, shouted toward the rider. "Hoodoo Dunn! You son-of-a-bitch!"

Tallman leaped from the chestnut, snatching Jake's Winchester as he went. But he still couldn't see the pair of stage robbers.

"Doc!" Tallman shouted, hoping to enrage the killer. "What are you doin' up there? Pearl makin' you eat pussy? Or is she just kickin' you around like usual!"

"Fuck you!" Doc shouted as he popped up and fired three wild shots through the small pine trees.

Tallman leveled the Winchester on a firm branch and shouted again. "Hey Doc! Pearl told me you couldn't get it up! That true?"

Doc popped up again, but before he could fire, Tallman's rifle bucked and the top of Doc's head erupted in a red and gray mist.

Then, an instant later, he caught sight of Pearl's Stetson and rifle. Before he had time to blink a puff of gunsmoke appeared. He heard Jake's dappled gray squeal. He turned in time to see it lurch up on its hind legs and flip on its back. The ground shook when the beautiful horse hit.

Expecting another shot, he rolled to his right, fixing his eyes on the spot where he'd seen Pearl's hat.

"Damn," he muttered as he heard her ride off.

SEVENTEEN

Vivian was concerned that Tallman had not returned to Tucson. It was almost eight o'clock. And it didn't help her spirits any when she saw Judd Hall come through the casino door and walk straight toward Jarrott.

She was just scooping up dealer's winnings when the ugly tree-stump walked straight to her table.

"Mr. Traber wants to see you," Hall growled, his deep-set eyes dull with ignorance and meanness.

"Well, I'm working."

"Jarrott says so!" Hall grunted, his eyes dropping to her fleshy vee. "And Mr. Traber don't like to wait!"

Vivian looked toward Jarrott, who shrugged and then turned his back to her. Concerned that something had gone wrong with the stagecoach trap, she hesitated at first.

"Like I said, lady, Mr. Traber don't like to wait."

Vivian knew she could handle Traber and his

oddball sex habits, but she sensed that Judd Hall was inhuman, more dangerous than a coiled diamondback. She'd soon find that she had figured him right.

Hall said nothing as he escorted her to the buckboard, and, likewise, she remained silent on the short ride to Traber's home.

Once inside, she was somewhat relieved, because it appeared that Traber was simply planning to get his horns shaved.

"Hello, Floyd."

"Susanna," Traber said as he approached and put his arm around her. "Meet Cindy."

"Cindy," Vivian said as she nodded.

"Cindy's a little surprise," Traber said, as the pretty saloon girl stared at Vivian's bosom. "She knows how to please a woman."

"Floyd . . . I'm not much for women," Vivian insisted, recalling the double-ended wooden penis she'd seen in his closet of horrors.

"Now, now, Susanna," Traber said, like a schoolmaster scolding an errant student. "It won't hurt a bit. You don't have to do a thing but enjoy it."

"Floyd," Vivian protested.

"Come with me, girls," he said after shooting Vivian a brief but commanding eye.

Once in the bedroom, the saloon girl reached for Vivian, and started to breathe more heavily as soon as she began to unbutton Vivian's dress. Traber undressed quickly, leaving his clothing in a heap, and began to fumble with the strange girl's stays and buttons. Vivian noticed that Traber's meat was limp and shriveled. While he disgusted her, she was not distressed with the other woman. Though she preferred men, she had no moral problems with sexual gratification in any form, as long as both parties were willing.

"You have nice tits, Susanna," the girl said as she fondled them briefly.

Traber jerked Cindy's dress, corset and petticoats down with one frantic movement. The girl's small, hard breasts popped free, revealing large dark-brown circles and long, dark nipples.

After she'd stripped Vivian, Cindy fingered the tender slit between Vivian's legs and lowered her head to suck hard on a nipple.

"The bed, girls," Traber moaned, his hands sampling their fruit as they walked the five feet.

Traber pushed Vivian back onto the bed and got on himself, pulling the saloon girl into the pile. Then he greedily palmed, sucked, and fingered the two women, all the time his limp cock flopping from thigh to thigh. While Traber acted like a twelve-year-old set free at the candy counter, Vivian lay still, not knowing how to respond. Cindy was kissing her way down from Vivian's breasts, on a path toward the auburn triangle that covered her womanhood.

Then Traber stood up, as Cindy positioned herself between Vivian's spread legs, pushed Vivian's thighs perpendicular to the bed, and lowered her hands to the swelling slit. Vivian shuddered, quickly becoming lost in the experience as Cindy grasped the pink petals, pushed them aside, and pushed her mouth into the moist bog, her tongue stabbing deep into the pulsating flesh. The girl's tongue expertly snaked in and out of the opening as Vivian began a rhythmic bucking which increased in tempo as the trained tongue of the queer saloon girl thrust deeper and faster. Her eyes closed, Vivian savored the strange experience as waves of pleasure began to flood her loins. On the edge of release, she grasped the girl's head and held her face in place and made little grunting sounds as she reached the pinnacle of her ecstasy and flooded Cindy's face with love juice.

"Damn! . . . Damn nice," Traber wheezed as he watched Vivian's orgasm.

Vivian opened her eyes, quickly regaining her composure. Traber stood above her, his limp cock dangling from his skinny body.

"You like that, Floyd?" Cindy asked as she lapped the juices from Vivian's crotch. "Did I do good?"

Traber didn't answer, his face a mask. He turned on his bony heel, went to the closet, and emerged with a small whip for each of the girls.

"Get up," he ordered.

Before Vivian had a chance to comprehend the moment, Cindy popped out of bed and took the whips, giving one to Vivian.

Crack.

The first stroke she laid on his taut ass sounded like .22-caliber gunfire.

Snap. She hit the front of his legs just below his meat.

Crack. And she left a red stripe on his white ass.

"You," Traber grunted, looking at Vivian. "Hit me."

Vivian took the whip and laced the beanpole vice boss on the back. Cindy was now laying softer strokes on his penis, which was swelling with desire. After several strokes, a bright red head popped out of his baggy foreskin.

"Harder!" he demanded as he took the hard-on in his fist and began pumping the eight-inch rod, which looked grossly out of proportion to the rest of his body.

The two girls continued to whip him as he danced in pain, jolted about the room by the whipstrokes, pounding his own long shaft.

The lashing grew in intensity and Vivian was truly tiring when he began to grunt and splash his seed on the floor.

"Stop," the queer saloon girl said. "He's going."

With a pained look he hammered his cock until the last drop ran down his hand. Then he fell on the bed.

"You two sleep here tonight," he sighed as he slapped the sheets on each side.

The two naked women exchanged a quick glance of disgust and then complied.

For more than an hour, Vivian lay awake, worrying about Tallman and waiting for Traber and the girl to fall into a deep sleep so that she could get away.

As she was lying there nude, the bullet-marked stage was a half hour out of Tucson, coming slowly with its morbid cargo, three dead outlaws and a dead Wells Fargo guard. The rain had started, a steady downpour.

In order to check, she rolled abruptly in the bed. Neither the firm-bodied saloon girl or Traber said anything or seemed to stir.

"Asleep," she said.

Neither answered.

Still nude, she slipped from the bed and stood quietly over the silent pair. Assured that they were asleep, she poked her head through the door and surveyed the hallway. Nothing stirred.

Her soft steps and an occasional creak in the floor were muffled by the drumming of the rain on the wooden shingles. She turned into Traber's study and stood quietly for a moment. Not hearing a sound, she closed the door and walked to his desk. She lit a match and put the kerosene lamp as low as it would go. The light reminded her of her nudity and left her feeling vulnerable. She wished she'd brought the derringer.

The third drawer she checked yielded paydirt, a leather-bound ledger that appeared to be his personal record of collections and payoffs.

Judd Hall, who lived in a room in the attached carriage house, was cleaning his rifle when he saw the light and the nude silhouette of a woman. At first he sighed, thinking the boss was up to his odd tricks. For some reason, at that moment he recalled one smart-assed whore who had threatened to blackmail Traber the year before. Hall had raped her and then slowly beat her to death. But, after a minute of staring at the nude form, his addled mind comprehended that the light was in Traber's private office. He slid his Remington .36 revolver from its worn leather and snuck into the house.

Vivian gasped when she looked up to find herself staring at a pistol muzzle and the twisted face of Judd Hall.

"What the hell you doin' in here?" he growled, his eyes lapping her firm, upsloping breasts and the neat triangle of hair.

"Floyd sent me looking for ah . . . ah . . . another whip."

"Don't look like no whip to me," he grunted when he eyed the ledger. "Mr. Traber!" he shouted. "Mr. Traber? You in there!"

Vivian's heart pounded when she saw Traber run into the room tying his robe.

"What the—?" he said, his eyes glowing with surprise.

"Sorry, boss. But did you send her in here? Sorry to bother you, but it looked like she was snoopin'!"

Traber looked down and saw his open ledger. He walked up and slapped her so hard she toppled backward and fell spread-eagle. "What the hell are you doing in here?"

He reached down, grabbed her hair, pulled her upright, and punched her in the right breast.

Vivian bent double in pain and fell back again.

"I asked you, woman," he spat. "What were you doin' in my books?"

Vivian, dazed by the painful blow in the chest, sensed that she'd die unless she could come up with something.

"Just trying to get ahead, Floyd," she said, getting to her knees. "Jesus Christ. I just figured if I knew something, I might get a small piece of the action."

Traber was about to hit Vivian again when Cindy gasped at the sight from the office doorway.

"You go home," Traber said after he turned toward the sound. "And remember! You haven't been here tonight!"

Vivian had gotten to her feet, and her eyes pleaded for help from Cindy.

"I haven't been here," she said as she abruptly broke Vivian's gaze and darted toward the bedroom.

"Wait until the skinny bitch is gone, Judd. Then bring this whore into the bedroom," Traber said as he turned to leave. "We'll find out what she's up to."

Hall, smelling like a two-day-old corpse, grabbed her arm, twisted it behind her back, and stuck his revolver in his belt. "You're going to be fun," he said as he torqued her arm further and squeezed her nipples with his free hand.

"You scum," Vivian spat.

Then she screamed as he bent her arm just short of the breaking point and squeezed her breast with a viselike grip. "We'll see who's going to die . . . *bitch.*"

After the frightened saloon girl scurried by half-dressed, Hall walked Vivian into the bedroom.

"Tie her to the bed, Judd, and find out why she's here."

"I told you why, Floyd," she pleaded. "I want in!"

Traber simply pulled out the four velvet-lined shackles that were chained to the bed and nodded to Hall, who then shoved Vivian to the bed and put his knee in her belly. When she tried to fight, Hall punched her in the temple with his fist.

She looked up and saw Traber's sharp angled face through a haze. Then his form became clear. Her head pounded with pain. Conscious again, she jerked her arms and legs. She was secured to the four posts of the bed. Her head hurt so badly that she could hardly think.

"Now tell me what the hell you're doing here. Make it easy on yourself, Susanna . . . or whoever you are."

"I told you—"

Traber nodded and Hall slapped her breasts with a leather riding crop. Her flesh quivered and turned pink instantly. Her mind was swimming. She was drowning, and it seemed that nothing would save her but some story that would make her an undisputable link in a takeover.

"You perverted slime," she said. Then she spat at him. "I'm not telling you a goddamn thing. But you can be sure that your days as king of the hill are numbered, and—"

Hall whipped her again, twice on the face.

"Ahhh," she groaned. "And when my friends find out about this, you're going to be strung up by that rubbery cock of yours."

Hall punched her in the belly.

"Just who are your friends?"

"Shit in your hat, you nutless slit," she growled as spittle and vomit dripped from the corner of her mouth.

Hall raised his fist to punch her again when Traber stopped him.

"Not so fast, Judd," he said as he walked to his closet. "Let's go slowly."

"I wanna kill this bitch, Mr. Traber."

"I understand, Judd. But let's do it slowly. It's more fun that way." He walked toward the bed with a wooden-handled whip that had twenty-two-foot leather thongs. "We'll take her hide slowly."

Hall laughed like an imbecile and took the whip.

As Traber stood over the bed with a crazed look on his face, Hall stroked Vivian lightly with the deadly device, which would slowly peel her hide.

"That's right, Judd. Start easy. We got all night."

EIGHTEEN

At almost the same moment Vivian had discovered the ledger, Tallman came through the door of the Wells Fargo office.

"Did you get the bastards?" Oldham asked eagerly.

"All but one," Tallman said as he slapped his soggy Stetson on his leg. "Goddamn woman got away."

"Jesus. What'll we do now?"

"Stay loose, Perry. I've got a new plan. We'll just go fishing again."

"Where are the outlaws you captured?" Oldham asked, his voice weary from lack of sleep.

Two of the Wells Fargo Express guards came in at that moment, and lowered their eyes when they saw Oldham.

"What happened?" he demanded.

"Lost Merlin," one guard said, his voice almost inaudible. "Sorry, boss."

"The woman shot him," Tallman added. "He never knew what happened."

"But we got the others, boss," the same guard added. "All three toes-up and on their way to Willingham's Funeral Parlor this very minute."

His broad shoulders sagged under the weight of his loss. "God," he sighed. "We've lost five good men and Wes is crippled and still might die."

"We're dealing with low-life, Perry," Tallman added. "I'm sorry."

Oldham asked for details and Tallman recounted the whole story, including the unfortunate escape of Pearl Bowen.

"I'll wire headquarters," he said, after listening to the tale. "I'm going to try to get authority to keep you on this case if it takes ten goddamned years. I want Pearl Bowen's hide nailed to a barn door."

"Hang on to your britches, Perry. We'll get Pearl. But in the meantime I want Jarrott. He's next up the line," Tallman said. "He's facing the gallows on conspiracy to commit murder. He'll talk rather than dance before the good folks of Tucson. We'll promise him that we'll put in a good word with the judge."

"Why not Traber?" Oldham shouted as he popped out of the chair. "Let's quit messing around. I can't keep those two tied up in the broom closet forever. We've lost that bitch killer, let's not risk losing the mastermind!"

While they argued the issue, the third express guard returned and reported that each of the three outlaws was at rest in a three-dollar pine box, ready for a trip to pauper's hill. Oldham began to argue that all six of them ought to go for Traber. But Tallman insisted that he would be more effective alone.

"Well shit on my bootheel," Oldham finally sighed. "You're the expert. Do it your way. But I'm telling you, I'm coming with my men if this isn't tied up by nine o'clock tomorrow morning."

Tallman gave Oldham a thin smile, but his eyes revealed his distaste for Oldham's idea of a frontal assault. He stood quietly, lit a cheroot, and walked toward the door, talking as he left, his back to the Wells Fargo district manager.

"Perry, you kill Jarrott, or Traber, or anyone else for that matter, and you'll be the one swinging. You will look mighty sheepish in court without one thread of evidence. Keep in mind who's running this town." The door closed with a thud.

Tallman slapped through the mud as he crossed to the plankwalk on the other side of the street, his head tilted into the heavy rain. He was relieved that Oldham wasn't going to launch a frontal assault on the Buena Suerte. That would have meant big trouble.

After a short, soggy walk, he'd made his way to the casino. Once inside he shook off his rain slicker and panned the room, looking for Vivian. He spotted Jarrott's bald head circulating in the crowd and assumed that he had no knowledge of the botched holdup. Tallman gave it a half hour. The word would spread like wildfire, as the stage robberies had become a major topic of barroom prattle. To many, those sour souls who devote their energy to blaming others for their own bungled lives, the stage robbers had become heroes who heaped a welcome misery on the bankers, the merchants, and Wells Fargo.

"Whiskey," he said as he bellied up to the bar.

"You look like a drowned cat, mister," the barkeep said in jest as he poured a shot so full it flowed over the glass.

"Feel like one," Tallman said after he bolted the cheap whiskey and planted the glass. "Do that again."

As the bartender poured, a scantily clad drink hustler approached. "Buy a girl a drink?" she asked.

"And one for the lady," Tallman added.

"Your usual, Melinda?" the barman asked.

"Sure."

He poured sugar water from a brand-name tequila bottle.

"Thought I'd visit that bitch, Lady Luck. See what she's got in store for me," he said as he sipped his second shot, and eyed her sagging breasts. "But I don't see my favorite dealer."

"Who's that?"

"The lady dealer."

"You too!"

"What?"

"She's got all you dudes going. Girl can't hardly make a living in here since Susanna snaked into town."

"She ain't workin' tonight?" Tallman asked.

"Night off. No doubt she still gets her pay, though."

"Damn, thought she said Thursday was her night off," Tallman sighed.

"It is. But lately it's any night Traber wants to play his fruity games."

"Goddamn!" Tallman exclaimed. "Traber! She's movin' fast."

"You got that square, cowboy. And old Sherm just weasels every time that creep Judd Hall wags his finger at Susanna."

"Again tonight?"

"Yeah. 'Course, truth be known, I don't envy her none over at Traber's house. We hear stories. A real cockroach. He can't do like most men, if you get my drift."

Tallman raised his eyebrows and sipped. He was suddenly concerned about Vivian. With Pearl loose, anything could happen. Even though Hoodoo Dunn had no connection with Susanna Duncan, Traber would look at every angle when he found out about the foiled robbery.

"Speakin' of doin' like a man," the bargirl said as she moved close enough to squish her soft drooping breasts on Tallman's arm. "I'll be off in a couple of hours, maybe by two or three."

"Well, now," Tallman said with a smile. "I just might take you out for an early breakfast. But first I'm goin' to my room to get out of these here soggy duds."

He tipped his wet hat and walked toward the front door. Out of the corner of his eye, he saw the floor manager, Obie Stallybrass, coming down the stairs like a man running from fire. Tallman turned, stopped, and pulled a slender cigar from his shirt pocket. The hurried man made his way quickly toward Jarrott through the loud and beligerent crowd. Once he had the casino owner's attention, he jabbered wildly and pointed up to the balcony that overlooked the floor.

Jarrott's expression turned sour and he headed for the stairs.

Tallman stepped onto the boardwalk and quickly assessed his options. Although it could have been something else, something told Tallman that Jarrott was, at that moment, learning of the stage ambush, probably from one of Traber's people. If Traber knew, Vivian might be in trouble.

Tallman made a snap decision and set off on a run toward Traber's house.

NINETEEN

While Jarrott ran up his stairs, across town, Traber and Hall had decided that flogging their captive was getting them nowhere. So Hall was heating a spoon over the chimney on the kerosene lamp. "Can we start with them titties?" Hall asked his crazed master, with a maniacal smile.

"Why sure, Judd. Not too hot at first."

Vivian's heart pounded at the thought of being disfigured by Hall's hot spoon.

Jarrott bolted through his office door. "What the hell are you doin' here?" he commanded.

"*We* got trouble. The stage job went sour today. Doc, Kirk, and Jake are all dead."

Jarrott was thinking, rubbing his chin. "That's good."

"Good!" Pearl shouted. "You fuckin' crazy!"

"Good that there's no witnesses, Pearl," he added

quickly. He knew Pearl was a cold-blooded murderess, and his mind had already conceived the fact that heads were going to roll when Traber found out. "Calm down and tell me what the hell happened."

"Probably a Pinkerton or a Wells Fargo undercover agent. Some slick who called himself Hoodoo Dunn helped us on the last job. It was him who led the ambush. And he ain't no amateur. They opened fire and killed Jake and Kirk right off. I shot some big son-of-a-bitch who was ridin' shotgun." Her eyes twinkled as she told Jarrott the details of her head shot. "Fuckin' nice shot," she repeated three times.

Jarrott moved to his desk, sat down, and quickly assessed his predicament. If Dunn, the undercover man, had gotten inside, someone else had to be inside the operation unless one of the three dead outlaws had talked.

"Any of your people have a loose tongue?"

"I'd bet against it," Pearl said.

"How did this son-of-a-bitch get inside, then? Nobody knew about this but me, my contact at Wells Fargo, and you. No one!"

"Bullshit," Pearl growled. "That bastard Hoodoo Dunn didn't appear out of the goddamn thin air."

"Were you followed?" Jarrott asked, wiping beads of sweat from his almost bald head.

"No."

"Sure?"

Pearl answered with her best murderer's eyes.

"Got someplace to hide?"

"Yeah, Sherm. Right here."

"That's no good!"

"It'll do just fine," she argued. "They won't be lookin' under their noses right off."

Jarrott didn't answer. He was thinking of the money he had in his safe. Forty-five thousand would make a fresh start up in Montana or somewhere else out of the way. He was smart enough to realize that a rattlesnake like Traber wouldn't give him one second of consideration if something should happen. He would kill his Wells Fargo Judas and then Jarrott himself. And that would leave Traber in the clear.

His other option, he thought to himself, was to kill Pearl, but he knew she was as quick as Traber, and that she was probably ready to gun him down if he even looked like he was going to move the wrong way.

"Best thing we can do, Pearl, is hold still and not do anything foolish," Jarrott stalled. "You stay here tonight and we'll find out how the cards are falling before we move."

He'd decided he'd kill her the first chance he got.

"Maybe we can even spend a night like old times," he added, remembering her lustful ways.

"This ain't no time to be playin', Sherm. We're in deep shit."

Tallman sloshed through the puddles at the side of Traber's house. At a dark window he listened. At first it was quiet. Then he heard a guttural cry, the sound of someone in pain who'd resigned themselves to the end. It had to be Vivian.

He scurried to the back door and, as he picked at the simple lock, he heard a voice.

"Now. Maybe you can tell us what we wanna know," Hall said with a white pasty drool in the corners of his mouth as he reheated the spoon. "This time I think I'll seal off that nipple for you. Burn it right off."

Vivian cranked her neck, looked at the spoon, which was glowing red. Hall had burned her twice but so far he hadn't disfigured her. At the sight of the glow she went slack.

She turned to Traber on the other side of the bed to say something, but saw he was in a trance. His robe was open and he was playing with his hard thick cock, pulling it in long, slow strokes.

Hall kept heating the spoon with his right hand. "I'll start with this one," he said as he pulled hard on her left nipple. "Burn that son-of-a-bitch right off. Bet you think you're pretty, don't you, bitch! You'll be workin' the sideshow when we're finished with you, slut. That is, if you're alive. Right, boss?"

"Yeah," Traber groaned as he picked up the tempo of his strokes.

"One more time, bitch," Hall growled, his spittle foaming. "Who are you workin' for?" he said as he removed the glowing spoon from the lamp chimney and positioned it an inch above her nipple.

Vivian felt the heat and her nipple became warm. She spat in his face, sending a gooey load of spit and bile into his left eye.

Hall backed up, closing his eyes.

"Burn her," Traber shouted as he stroked harder. "Burn her tit, Judd!"

"Sorry to interrupt your little party," a voice growled. Tallman filled the bedroom doorway.

Hall dropped the spoon and went for the Colt he'd stuffed in his belt.

Before the spoon hit the carpet, Tallman had fired three shots from his .41. The blast from the quicksilver-filled slugs caught the thug in the gut, chest, and Adam's Apple, sprayed a mist of gore and sent Hall down as if his legs had been chopped away at the knees. He hit with a thud. Though the bodyguard was twitching wildly he was dead.

"Ash," Vivian shouted.

Tallman looked over and saw rage on her face. Then he saw Traber. His eyes widened in disbelief. He was pulling his cock faster than ever as he stared at Hall's dead eyes and ruptured gut and chest.

"Kill him," Vivian shouted as she strained at the chains. "Kill'm."

Tallman, taken aback by Traber, hesitated and then unlatched the shackles.

Traber groaned as his hand moved like the engine connecting rod on a downhill train. His seed shot upward and out, a large glob landing on Hall's gray cheek.

Vivian untied her last thong and struggled out of bed. She ran at Traber and kicked him. The top of her bare foot caught him in the balls and lifted him off the floor.

The skinny kingpin went down like he'd been shot.

"Vivian," Tallman said, still at a loss.

"Slime," she shouted as she stomped on his face with her heel. "You son-of-a-bitch," she cried as she scrambled at her clothing, coming up with her derringer.

"Vivian!" Tallman shouted as he reached for the small gun that was pointed at Traber's crotch.

"Vivian," he said as he firmly grasped her hand and she moved the gun away from the squirming snake on the floor. "We need him."

Vivian loosened her grip and let Tallman take the derringer. She wanted to encircle him with her arms and cry for two hours, but she bit her lip and held strong. Pinkerton agents didn't cry.

"Jesus Christ, Viv," Tallman said as he looked down. Her whole body from her knees to her face was crisscrossed with red welts, several of which were seeping blood. Catching his eyes, she looked down too and cradled her breast and examined the two minor burns.

"Jesus, Viv. I'm sorry."

"I'll heal. Just be glad you got here when you did. They were about to get rough. He was about to scar me for life."

"Traber," Tallman said as he looked toward the skinny pervert as Vivian began to dress. "You'd better pray you hang. 'Cause if you don't, I'm going to show you how the Indians can take five days to kill a man."

TWENTY

Oldham opened the door at the Wells Fargo office, and Tallman shoved a humped-over Floyd Traber through the door so hard that he stumbled and fell. Oldham was taken aback by the sight of Tucson's number-one tough nut cowering on his side. Then he saw Vivian.

"My God!" he gasped when he saw the raised welts on her neck and upper chest. "What the . . ."

"Our big man here whips women," Tallman growled, his tone revealing a willingness to cut Traber's throat on the spot. "If we didn't need him, I'd take him into the desert and show him a few Indian tricks I know."

"Never mind, Mr. Oldham," Vivian said, holding up the leather-faced ledger. The prospect of a major arrest on her second assignment somewhat soothed her bruised and scorched skin. "He'll put on quite a show in front of the courthouse—dancing on air."

Tallman had an image of Traber pulling his meat while he strangled, the ultimate orgasm.

"Hangin's too good for this joker," one of the express guards muttered as he unsheathed a large dirk. "We ought to take his balls right now and make him eat them."

"He'd probably enjoy it," Vivian said, remembering his outrageous behavior and forgetting present company. "He'd likely pull his pud while you were cutting."

At once, the stage driver, the three express guards, Oldham, and Tallman looked at Vivian with raised eyebrows. Tallman was smiling, remembering his hanging image.

"What can I tell you! The creep is perverted," she said.

They all stood quietly, each momentarily taken with their thoughts of what the lady Pinkerton must have endured earlier that evening and oddly amused at her ability to hang tough at a time when most women and many men would be whimpering with despair.

Tallman reached down, grabbed Traber's forearm, snatched the vice boss to his feet, and shoved him backward into a chair, thus breaking the silence in the room.

"Perry, get that Judas clerk of yours," Tallman said, keeping his eyes on Traber. "Let's clear this up."

Oldham left the outer office, and Vivian began to carefully examine the well-kept ledger.

"Well, now, Traber," Tallman said, tipping back his damp Stetson as Oldham entered with the pale, frightened clerk. "What we have here is someone who's going to tell the judge that he fed you information you used to rob Wells Fargo and, more important, information you used to kill five men."

"And to shoot another in the nuts," one of the express guards broke in.

"I don't know this man," Traber insisted. "You're crazy. And the Tucson sheriff doesn't cotton to kidnapping."

"Don't be simpleminded, Traber," Tallman went on. "We have an eyewitness who saw this clerk deliver the time and the type of shipment on this morning's nine o'clock stage. We've already got a signed confession. And your gang is dead!"

Oldham took the handwritten document and thrust it in Traber's face.

"I've never talked to this man in my life," Traber shot back, now hoping only to get to the sheriff's office alive. He knew Tucson's top lawdog was in as deep as the rest of them.

"I gave my information to Hall," the clerk insisted.

"And Hall's dead," Traber said with a smile.

"Here it is, Ash," Vivian broke in. "I already have three entries to a B. Harkins. Five hundred dollars each time. And—"

"You low-life!" Oldham shouted at his clerk, as he shook the traitor. "I still can't believe you sold those men's lives for five hundred dollars."

"Easy, Perry," Tallman said. Then he turned to Traber. "See there, your own little book's going to put the noose around your neck." He turned back to Oldham. "Put Harkins back in the closet and bring in Westfall."

Traber's jaw dropped.

"Like you thought, Ash," Vivian said while Oldham was fetching the mayor. "The sheriff's on the take too. Matter of fact, looks like half the damn town's suckin' on Traber's teat."

"What about Judge Vogt, the federal district court judge?" Tallman asked.

"Nothing yet," she said, her eyes still scanning the ledger.

"I think he's clean," Tallman added. "Unless you find otherwise, we'll drag this sack of snakes over to his place when we're done."

Traber's eyes fell to his lap and he became acutely aware of his aching balls.

Next, Tallman confronted Traber with the blubbery Westfall, who, although having no direct knowledge of the stage robberies, was singing like a bird. Then Tallman confronted Traber with an option: "Confess or hang."

Hoping for the best and fully aware that he had nothing on the Territorial judge, Francis Vogt, he spilled his guts while Vivian carefully copied the details. Traber signed each page of the confession and Vivian then handed it and the ledger to Perry Oldham, who placed it on the desk next to the confessions of the clerk and the mayor.

"That's that," Vivian said, her wounds becoming more painful in her tight clothing.

"What about Pearl Bowen?" Oldham injected. "I want that ruthless bitch to hang."

"We haven't forgotten Pearl," Tallman said. "Jarrott will likely know where she is. Right now, I want you and your men to rope these three bums together and take them to Judge Vogt's house."

"It's two in the mornin'," one of the express guards grunted.

"Judge won't mind," Tallman said to the guard. He went on. "Show the judge the ledger and the confessions and explain why we didn't go to the sheriff. He'll probably deputize you until he clears things up. Vivian and I are going to visit with Mr. Jarrott."

Tallman and Vivian entered the Buena Suerte less than a minute apart. The crowd was thinning and the tables and bar were occupied mostly by an assortment of bums and hard cases who were saturated with pop-skull whiskey. The piano player and the banjo plucker had lost their verve. The bass player was gone.

"Where's Sherm?" she asked the bartender as she shook the wet rainslicker she'd borrowed from one of the express guards in order to cover her lash marks.

The barkeep pointed toward the balcony suite. Vivian looked toward Tallman. They met at the stairs and Tallman unholstered his Colt and dropped another deadly load in the empty chamber.

Vivian knocked when they reached the door.

"Yeah. Who is it?" They heard from the room after several moments of silence.

"Susanna."

"Be down in a minute. Doin' some bookwork."

"Traber sent me with a message," Vivian insisted.

"Just a minute."

The door opened and Tallman, his Colt cocked, brushed past Vivian and leveled his revolver on Jarrott.

"What the hell!" Jarrott gasped. "Why, you goddamn bitch!" he shouted when he saw Vivian. His first thought was that Tallman had been sent by Traber to silence him.

"After we have a little talk, Jarrott, we're going to take a walk over to Judge Vogt's so you can join the rest of Tucson's most prominent coyotes."

"Who the hell. . . ."

"Pinkertons," Vivian interrupted proudly.

"You goddamn slut!"

Like a lightning bolt, Tallman reached out with his Colt and hit Jarrott on the chin with his Colt barrel. He'd heard and seen all the abuse of Vivian that he could handle.

Jarrott shouted another curse despite the deep one-inch gash on his cheekbone. Tallman planted his left palm in Jarrott's chest and sent him reeling backward into his expensive sofa.

"You're expendable," Tallman said, his voice still showing the renewed rage he felt over Vivian's ordeal. "Traber, the mayor and the Wells Fargo clerk are all singing a nice melody for Judge Vogt this very minute. So we don't need you." Tallman took two steps and put the big-bore barrel six inches from the bridge of Jarrott's nose. "There's only one loose end, and that's Pearl Bowen. She wouldn't risk going to the cabin. So you tell me where to look, or we'll save the taxpayers their court costs in your case!"

"Look over your shoulder, shit-for-brains. You cocksucker, Hoodoo Dunn—or whoever you are."

The room went still. Jarrott eyeballed Tallman's Colt and Tallman turned to see Pearl's .44 Bulldog pointed at his skull.

"Well, I'll be damned. If it ain't Momma. Surprised you're not back suckin' and fuckin' your kiddies!" Tallman said, hoping insults would delay her obvious intentions. "Oh, that's right—they're all dead. Damn, I bet it'll take a while to find three more dimwitted peckerwoods like them."

"You shut up, asshole!"

" 'Course if you can't get a man any other way. I guess you do what you have to."

Vivian saw the blood in Pearl's eyes and knew she could shoot Tallman in the head without one twitch of her eyes or the slightest remorse.

"Say goodbye, Pinkerton," Pearl growled.

Vivian screamed and dove for the floor behind Jarrott's desk, clawing for the derringer strapped to her thigh.

Distracted, Pearl fired. Her slug splintered the top left corner of the desk. Tallman spun away from Pearl's sights, seeing from the corner of his eyes that Jarrott's hand was going into his jacket.

Before Tallman could level his .41, Pearl had thumbed another chamber into place.

Going for broke, Vivian popped up with her derringer and fired one shot into Pearl's left breast. The quicksilver-filled lead exploded in her chest, jolting the wide-eyed killer from her feet. She fell in a heap, her mouth gurgling like she was drowning.

An instant after the explosion, Tallman, still spinning away, dove for the floor. Jarrott's small-caliber vest gun cracked and Tallman felt suddenly like he'd been kicked in the thigh by a wild horse. Vivian turned toward the sharp report of Jarrott's hideout gun and fired her second barrel, hitting Jarrott in the side just before his small revolver cracked again. Tallman heard Jarrott's second slug thunk in the wall behind his head just as he fired his Colt, slamming three deadly rounds into Jarrott's vest. The casino owner's body jumped on the couch in a macabre dance as each slug found its mark.

Then the room was quiet except for Pearl's labored breathing, her lungs pumping red-purple bubbles on her blood-saturated shirt. The air was thick with the acrid odor of gunsmoke and the sickening stench of blood.

"Ash," Vivian groaned, when she saw the puddle of bright red blood under his leg. Suddenly aware of his wound, she rushed to his side.

"Nothing to brag about," Tallman said of the pumping wound.

Vivian fumbled for Tallman's boot knife. Then she cut his pants and ripped a piece from the hem of her wet and wrinkled dress. "In and out," she said when she saw the clean small wound in the fleshy part of his thigh. The exit wound was worse than she'd let on.

Then she sighed with relief after stopping the blood with a tight wrap, and slumped against the wall. Both of the Pinkertons were, at once, acutely aware of the devastation that lay at their feet. Then, a sound at their right caused Tallman to instinctively point his revolver. It was Pearl. As her leg flexed up and down, she turned her glassy eyes on the detectives. She moved her mouth as if to curse them both, but nothing came out. Then her leg went straight and she began to gasp and spit blood. Air whistled through the hole in her chest in a final long breath. Her legs went stiff and then slackened as one bootheel drummed four rhythmic beats on the wood floor. The smell of urine permeated the air.

Vivian turned away from the dead woman only to see Jarrott upright in the sofa, his mouth drooping open, his glasses askew, and his eyes focused on infinity. She would have started to cry over the gross deaths, her own throbbing wounds, and her bloody partner, but the fear-stricken floor manager crashed through the door with a double-barreled scattergun, tripped over Pearl's body, dropped his shotgun, and went careening toward the sofa and landed in Jarrott's lap.

When she saw the absolute horror in the eyes of Obie Stallybrass, she fell victim to a state of unchecked morbid laughter.

"Do me a favor," Tallman said nonchalantly to the horror-struck casino manager. "Think you can quit pitchin' woo to your boyfriend there long enough to go fetch Judge Vogt? He'll understand! And get me a doctor."

Vivian's tearful laughter was infectious, and Tallman began to shake with belly-cramping hilarity as the bugeyed Obie Stallybrass dashed from the absurd scene.

TWENTY-ONE

Tallman squinted in the bright sunlight as he stepped down from the hansom cab and turned to take Vivian's outstretched hand. Chicago's Washington Street was crowded with finely attired ladies under parasols and expensively suited men of all descriptions.

After Vivian had stepped down, Tallman fingered a silver dollar from his vest pocket and paid the driver, who got wide-eyed over the four-bit tip.

No one strolling the granite-block Chicago sidewalk would have imagined that the pair had just returned from a savage land. Tallman could easily have been mistaken for a successful lawyer, and Vivian looked as if she might be chairwoman of the Chicago Concert Society.

"Here we are," Tallman said as they turned to face the imposing four-story brick structure.

Vivian, looking exceptionally refined in her

reserved but finely cut dark-blue dress, nodded her approval.

Allan Pinkerton will be impressed, Tallman thought to himself as he limped through the carved oak door, which swung on heavy hammered-brass hinges. He had rarely seen her in a dress that covered her to the neck, and he liked it.

Gold-leaf scrollwork on a heavy frosted-glass door announced the PINKERTON DETECTIVE AGENCY.

"Good morning, Mr. Tallman," the young receptionist said, eyes and teeth gleaming.

"Myrna. Good to see you," he said as he doffed his fedora. "You're looking fit."

Myrna, a pert blonde with kewpie-doll features, batted her lashes and glowed. Then she saw Vivian come into full view.

"Myrna. I'd like you to meet Vivian Valentine, one of the firm's newest agents."

"Pleased to meet you," the secretary responded, her voice, in fact, revealing displeasure. "Mr. Pinkerton is expecting the both of you." Her tone was suddenly very businesslike. "Go right in."

Vivian shot Tallman a playful reprimand as he limped toward the inner office.

As they entered the plain but functional office, the famous detective popped out of his chair, circled his desk, and extended his hand toward Vivian.

"Miss Valentine. An honest pleasure, to be sure." His mood was ebullient.

Tallman smiled inwardly. More often than not,

his meetings were with a peevish Allan Pinkerton who was forever intent on reprimanding him for his unruly behavior.

"*My* pleasure," Vivian responded, her eyes the focus of her inviting beauty.

"Ashley," Pinkerton said as he released Vivian's hand and directed it toward his most errant employee. "Fine job in Tucson."

Tallman raised his eyebrows and imagined that Pinkerton's handshake and tone were a little more sincere this time. He even thought he detected a smile beaming through the man's thick salt-and-pepper beard. "Why thanks, Allan," he replied. "It did get nasty toward the end."

While Pinkerton dropped into a wingback chair, Tallman and Vivian settled on a sofa that was trimmed in hand-carved walnut.

"*Both* of you are to be commended for your work in Tucson," Pinkerton said as he scooted the chair toward his desk. "I've received wires from Mr. Oldham, the newly appointed sheriff, and the chairman of the board of Wells Fargo. They all heaped praise on you. In fact, the chairman of Wells Fargo insisted that you, as a team, handle any further work they have." Pinkerton's eyes dropped and his voice became quieter. "Mr. Oldham briefly explained your ordeal . . . ahhh . . . Miss . . . ahhh . . . Valentine. And . . . ah . . . I must say you have shown a degree of courage which reflects favorably on the agency."

"Thank you, Mr. Pinkerton," Vivian said, truly

appreciating the praise. As a con artist, her work had been acknowledged only by the penalty of the law. Honest gratitude from one of America's best-known men gave her a new sense of pride. Then she thought of Tallman. "Of course, Ashley's wound is no small matter."

"Of course! *Of course!*" Pinkerton said as he pushed aside a stack of papers and looked toward Tallman.

"What did the sheriff have to say?" Tallman asked, intent on keeping tabs on Traber's fate. "Have they had the trial yet?"

"Next week," Pinkerton said in a matter-of-fact voice. "He expects that Traber and the express clerk will hang before the end of the month."

Tallman was relieved at the news. Then his eyes caught a flashing glance from Vivian and they began to snicker. During the train trip back to Chicago, they had gone into several fits of laughter over Vivian's explicit imitations of Floyd Traber pounding his meat as he went through the trapdoor.

Pinkerton raised his bushy eyebrows and dropped his jaw, taken aback as the two detectives seemingly laughed raucously over a double hanging.

"Private joke, chief," Tallman said, checking his laughter when he saw Pinkerton's surprise. "Floyd Traber has several humorous idiosyncrasies."

Vivian laughed again and Tallman chimed in. Pinkerton sighed and his shoulders sagged as he stroked his beard, his eyes revealing some minor distress. Vivian Valentine would not be one of his more manageable agents. He usually had his hands full with Tallman, and he pondered the possibility of trying to hold *a pair* of unruly agents in check. The thought of it almost made him wilt. Then he reminded himself of the large bank draft coming from Wells Fargo. The pair was damn near worth their weight in gold coin. Right then and there, as the pair chuckled over their private joke, he decided that he'd find some way to deal with them, even if the only solution was to let them dance to their own music.

"Well, chief," Tallman said, red-faced but quiet, and trying to get their meeting back on the tracks. "We are glad you were satisfied." He paused and gently slapped his knees as if to signal that he was about to get up. "Both of us need a little time to allow the wounds to heal. We figured to take off until the beginning of September. That's just under three weeks."

Pinkerton smiled through the full black-and-gray beard and tapped the fingers of his right hand on the mahogany desktop. Then he began flipping the pages of a calendar. "It's Friday," he said in a monotone. "Let's see." Pinkerton stopped on one of the pages, looked up, and eyed Tallman as a father might look at a disobedient son. "A week from Monday, you'll be on your way to Texas."

"Texas!"

"Yes, Texas! I need two good undercover operatives. And you're it. I've already promised the governor himself."

Vivian shrugged her shoulders and Tallman slumped back in his chair faking a look of disappointment. A week was more than he had hoped for. On the way over to the office, he had explained to Vivian that he would ask for three weeks, hoping for no more than three days. He didn't look in her direction, frightened that the laughter might break loose again.

"What calls us to Texas, Mr. Pinkerton?" Vivian asked.

"It seems as if we've got a nasty feud, which is on the verge of becoming a war. It started as a family vendetta. But it has developed into something much bigger."

"Sutton-Taylor?" Tallman butt in. Though not up on details, he was aware of the developing storm. "The newspaper scribblers are picking up on it. Especially since John Wesley Hardin sided with the Taylors. Noble outlaw with a cause!"

Vivian seemed surprised that Tallman had heard of the problem. She hadn't.

"What troubles the governor is that people *are* taking sides," Pinkerton said. "It's not just gunslicks like Hardin. Lawmen, judges, the large ranchers, and even the Texas Rangers are beginning to show sympathy with one side or the other."

"Where do we fit in?" Vivian asked.

"I want you to infiltrate both sides. Find out exactly what is going on so that I can report to the governor. Armed with that information, he will—with your help—attempt to bring the Sutton-Taylor mess to an abrupt conclusion."

"I hear they are playing for keeps down there," Tallman said as Pinkerton opened his bottom desk drawer.

The bearded, once-muscular hulk drew a large manila envelope from the drawer and thumped the heavy object on his desk. "Summary hangings, wild-eyed vigilantes, hired gunmen, local political skulduggery . . . you name it," the firm's founder said as he slid the package toward the front of the desk. "Our research people have prepared dossiers on the principals involved, and the governor has provided you with his suspicions and suggestions, written in his own hand. Right now, only four people in the world know about our prospective operation. Three of them are in this room." Pinkerton paused and gave each of the two detectives a stone-cold eye. "You are alone on this. And with killers like Hardin involved, I don't have to tell you that you'll not be on a picnic." He paused and leaned forward on his desk. "Add long-standing family feuding to man's routine evildoing and you have a situation that makes stagecoach robbery look like child's-play." He stared at Tallman only. "Brings out the worst in people. I am sure *you* understand that, Ashley."

"Been there before," Tallman said, making light of

Pinkerton's serious tone as he stood up and snatched the heavy envelope from the desk.

Vivian followed Tallman's lead and got up. After half a minute of small talk, they left the spartan office.

"Ashley," the secretary said as Vivian closed Pinkerton's door. "I have a message for you."

"Oh?"

"Aaron Wagner. He dropped us a note last week and requested that you go by his gun shop the next time you have a chance." She held out the note, her eyes fixed on his angular features. He took the note and kissed the back of her hand, allowing his gray-blue eyes to penetrate her psyche as if to say: *Some day, Myrna.*

After Vivian had climbed into a carriage they had flagged down, she reprimanded Tallman. "Shame on you! Using that pretty little mutt the way you do! She ought to be courting some bean-counter at one of the local accounting firms. As it is now, she'll stumble after you forever."

Tallman turned to his partner and grinned as he jammed a thin cigar between his square white teeth.

That settled, Vivian went on about how she had been embarrassed at their laughter. "I felt like a fool. But I couldn't help it," she said as the single Belgium clip-clopped along the city streets, its clean and brushed features flying with each powerful step.

She craned her neck to one side, held her right hand over her head as if she was gripping a rope, stuck out her tongue, rolled her eyes back, and pumped her hand up and down in her lap. The driver had turned around, and the sight almost caused him to fall from his hack. Bugeyed, he turned back to his horse and snapped the reins as if to escape an approaching highwayman.

In twenty minutes, the driver had made his way to the outskirts of the Chicago business district. He stopped in front of the small but neat store marked with a black-on-white sign: GUNSMITH, AARON WAGNER, PROP.

After he got his money, the driver gave the well-dressed duo a furtive glance and quickly urged his stout Belgium away from the curb.

"Ash!" the slender gunsmith said as he came from behind the counter with his hand extended. "Glad to see you!" Then he turned to Vivian. "And I bet this is Miss Valentine."

"Vivian," she replied, her tone sonorous, her eyes twinkling.

"Ash explained that he had a lady partner when he purchased a pair of .41 derringers. But he never let me in on the fact that she was one of the prettiest ladies in Chicago."

The gunsmith was obviously charmed by Vivian, and she, likewise, found Wagner to be a captivating gentleman. His eyes revealed intelligence and intensity and his clothing and heavy cotton apron were pressed and tidy. Though he was short, his coal-black hair, eyebrows, and stubby mustache gave him a classy appearance. He looked more like a successful commodities broker than an inventor and merchant of instruments of death.

"I got a message that you wanted to see me," Tallman said when he had regained Wagner's attention.

Wagner's eyes lit up like diamonds on black velvet. Without a word, he beckoned them to follow him into his workshop.

He reached up on a shelf and got down a cigar box. When he opened the wooden lid, Tallman saw twenty or thirty one-inch steel ball bearings bedded in snow-white cotton. Then he remembered that Wagner had explained during his last visit that he was working on a small impact grenade. Wagner plucked one of the small spheres from the box and headed toward the back door. "Follow me," he commanded, his tone and demeanor like that of a twelve-year-old showing his best friend the new .22 rifle he'd just gotten for Christmas. "You'll get a kick out of this, Ash!"

Once outside, Wagner turned and held the shiny metal ball aloft as a magician might hold up a silver dollar before making it disappear. Then he pointed at a full-length paper target mounted on thick oak planks that leaned on the six-foot fence enclosing his firing range and test area. Someone with no artistic ability had drawn a silhouette of a man on the stiff paper. The chest of the paper victim was full of large-caliber bullet holes. Without warning, Wagner drew back his arm and hurled the small bomb at the hard ground at the feet of the target. A simultaneous eruption of fire and an explosion not unlike the muzzle blast of a .60-caliber buffalo gun caused the two detectives to spin away and cover their eyes. Dirt and several slow-moving shards of steel fell on them in the aftermath of the demonstration.

As the smoke drifted over the fence, Wagner turned, his face aglow like that of a man viewing his newborn son.

"What do you think, Ash?"

Vivian and Tallman were speechless.

"Take a look," Wagner insisted as he set out toward the target, which was only twenty feet away. "The thing doesn't have any range, but up close it's got punch!"

The Pinkerton duo looked at each other with broad grins and followed. The legs of the figure on the paper target were peppered with metal splinters, saturated at the bottom, the concentration decreasing as their eyes moved higher.

"Ouch!" Vivian said, pointing to a large chunk of metal that was embedded in the vee of the target's crotch.

Wagner's face flushed to a pink glow. "Ah . . . yes . . . well, you can see that the grenade is not fatal if you throw it at your mark's feet."

"Depends on how you define *fatal*, Aaron!" Vivian exclaimed, giving Wagner a sly smile as she tapped the paper victim's crotch with her red fingernail. "Looks as if our friend here is out of the fight . . . *permanently!*"

The gunsmith's face went from pink to red and he quickly launched into an explanation of his new bomb. It was simply, he explained, one sphere within another. There was a sixteenth-of-an-inch space between the heavy-gauge steel outer shell and the thin tin inner ball. Wagner noted that he filled the inner sphere with a new high-velocity explosive developed by the Du Pont family in Wilmington, Delaware, and a flame-producing agent he'd concocted in his own lab. Once he'd sealed that, he'd filled the sixteenth-inch gap with fulminate of mercury. On impact, the fulminate exploded quickly and evenly, concentrating the force toward the center of the grenade. "It's that concentration of energy that produces such a violent detonation of the new high-velocity powder and my fire agent!"

Tallman looked up from the little crater at the victim's feet and eyed Wagner with some disbelief.

"Hardly something one could produce at a price the market would accept," Wagner went on. "The Du Pont powder is very expensive and still in experimental stages. And it takes hours to fabricate each of the double-sphere casings." He stopped and looked at Tallman. "And . . . of course . . . shipping would be a problem." His eyes then grew hopeful. "But one never knows what the future will hold, Ashley. And I wonder if you might have the opportunity to test my invention on some—ah—future assignment."

Tallman was thinking of Wagner's concern over shipping the bombs, when Vivian chimed in. "I wish we'd had these on the last job," she said as she again put her slender figure on the chunk of steel protruding from the target's crotch. "I'd like to have thrown one of these little gems at Floyd Traber while he was dancing around the room with his talleywhacker in his fist!"

Wagner's mouth dropped open.

"You will notice, Aaron, that Vivian speaks plainly," Tallman said as he put his arm around the five-and-a-half-foot inventor and moved him toward the shop.

Vivian smiled. She enjoyed getting a rise out of men with her unconventional behavior.

Back in the shop, after assurances from Wagner that the grenades would not go off at the slightest jostling in his pocket, Tallman agreed to carry six of the little bombs on his next assignment. Considering that they would have to walk naked into a hornet's neat within two weeks, they decided that *anything* he could bring along might help.

Both were tired and stuffed with German food and dark beer by the time they reached Tallman's hideaway just beyond Chicago's outskirts. As the carriage driver urged his Percheron away from the secluded stone dwelling, Tallman limped down the path toward the grove of trees that hid his home. He had told no one but his lawyer and Vivian about its existence. Pinkerton and his fellow agents had no knowledge of his private life, and he intended to keep it that way. He had always approached life with fierce independence as the foundation of his conduct. Except in rare cases where fate demanded otherwise, he held no man's marker, nor did he issue any. He'd held firm to the understanding that with people came problems. Therefore, it followed that minimum contact with others led to fewer problems. And, were it not for the fact that Vivian held a similar view of the cosmos, she wouldn't be following him up the path.

"Leg acting up?" she asked from behind.

"Not bad," he lied.

"I bet."

Once inside, she insisted that she change the dressing and examine the hole in his thigh.

Tallman limped into the bedroom and lay down on the bed. She put her things down and tugged off his boots, undid his trousers, and slid the blue pants from his legs.

The bandage was leaking, though not badly.

Vivian left the room and laid a fire in the kitchen cookstove, put on a pan of water, and laced it with Epsom salts crystals.

For the hour he lay on his stomach while she

applied hot compresses to the exit wound, he imagined that he was as content as any man.

Vivian was concerned over the wound, though she didn't show it. The front side was healing quickly, but the place where Jarrott's deformed bullet had come out had left several nasty triangular flaps of flesh. But she continued to make light of it and explained that she intended to keep him in bed for several days.

After she had sucked the pus out with the hot compresses, she applied some of the yellow powder the Tucson doctor had given her, and carefully bandaged the leg.

"All right, mister. You can roll over now. Your nurse is finished."

Tallman rolled to his back and watched as Vivian popped the cork on the champagne she'd iced right after she had fired up the stove. She poured two full glasses and handed one to Tallman after he had hoisted himself upright on two thick pillows.

"Here's to *us,*" he said as he clinked her glass and took a long pull on the bubbly wine. "*And* to a week of good food, rest, fine wine and all the other pleasures that the good Lord himself has heaped upon us!"

"Eat, drink and be merry," she said, lifting her glass over her head. "For some day we *will* die."

With that, Vivian took a sip of her champagne, turned, and disappeared into the guest room, which she had taken as her territory.

Before she had gone down the hallway, Tallman

had opened the large envelope. He thumbed through the dossiers until he saw one tagged: *John Wesley Hardin*. As he read that brief biography and subsequently two others, Vivian drew hot water from the stove, bathed, and dressed for bed.

When she finally appeared in the doorway in a sheer white silk gown she'd purchased their last day in Tucson, she looked like everyone's image of a Greek goddess.

Her auburn hair was down and brushed, and her breasts rested firmly under silk, sloping only slightly downward and out, faintly visible under the shiny garment. The kerosene lamp seemed to give her a ghostlike quality. After her pause in the doorway, she moved to the bed and took away his stack of files.

"No more work tonight!"

"Oh." Tallman grinned.

"Move over."

Tallman scooted over on the thick goosedown mattress. She issued a faint scent of orange blossoms, and the mere thought of what lay ahead caused his manhood to grow warm. She always approached sex as a hungry man might attack a steak dinner. No one could resist *that*. And she knew it.

Vivian got on her knees next to him, pulled his drawers down slowly, and flung them to the floor. Then she settled next to him, sought his mouth with her moist warm lips, and began gently probing with her tongue. The thought of nine days of fine food, expensive wine, and inventive sex made her damp with desire. As she kissed Tallman, she firmly encircled his cock with her slender fingers and gently pumped his throbbing erection while she fingered the tip with her index finger. Feeling his hips churning, she sensed that his first release would come quickly, allowing them to later get down to lingering and more satisfying sex.

She broke the kiss and moved to a kneeling position between his legs. Her hair fell to his thighs and stomach as she bent forward and took his swollen shaft in her mouth and swallowed to where her hand held the thick base of the throbbing cock. Barely allowing her teeth to graze the tight skin, she began to bob her head, blowing and sucking with each cycle.

On the edge, Tallman grasped her head in his palms and held her as he thrust upward while she sucked loudly, grunting animal noises.

Then, almost painfully, his seed surged through his cock in waves and filled her eager mouth. She slowed her sucking at the same falling tempo of his declining spasms. Then she gently lapped at the salty fluid which dripped from his stiff penis.

"God! I love the taste of a man!"

Tallman raised his head and watched as she lovingly lapped him. He knew that she wasn't lying as he shuddered under her trained tongue while she licked him to a higher level of bestial desire.

Seeing that he was ready again, she raised her head, flung her hair back and moved forward until she was straddling him. With her sheer gown bunched up on her hips, she lowered her hot, dripping slit onto his throbbing meat.

"Ahhhh . . . damn Ash!" she gasped. Her eyes were wide, her neck arched back, and her soft mouth was spread wide in a circle.

Tallman watched her breasts as they danced under silk and was, for an instant, in awe of her unchained desire. She jolted up and down in a sexual frenzy, grunting strange sounds, straining toward the moment when her flesh would tingle in ecstasy. He grabbed her hips, pulled her forward and pumped the both of them toward the peak. A moment later, locked together, they soared over the summit.

Vivian screamed his name in that last instant. Then she collapsed into his arms, exquisitely spent. Tallman pulled her close, and she tenderly pillowed her head on his shoulder.

They slept a dreamless sleep.